FOREV
YOUr

A Manual for Rejuvenation and Longevity

Gladys Iris Clark

FOREVER YOUNG

YOUNG

A Manual for Rejuvenation and Longevity

Gladys Iris Clark

 Published by Light Technology Publishing
P.O. Box 1526, Sedona, AZ 86339

FOREVER YOUNG

HOW TO ATTAIN LONGEVITY
Gladys Iris Clark

Previously Published by
Sun Publishing Company
P.O. Box 5588
Santa Fe, N.M. 87502-5588
ISBN: 0-89540-163-0

Published by
Light Technology Publishing
P.O. Box 1526
Sedona, AZ 86339

ISBN: 0-929385-53-5

Printed In the United States of America
Mission Possible Commercial Printing
P.O. Box 1495
Sedona, AZ 86339

10 9 8 7 6 5 4 3

✦DEDICATION✦

To Charles Henry, my golden companion and steadfast teacher.

To The Luminaries above and the L's below: Light, Life, Love, Laughter, Longing and Learning.

My grateful thanks to Geoffrey Stirling for his generous assistance in making this third printing of *FOREVER YOUNG* possible.

◆FOREWORD◆

There never was a time when my glorious Fantasies, which often became precious truths, were withheld. Having lived an unusually diverse and exciting life until this present moment, I wanted to share what I have learned, not only with friends, but with the whole world.

Therefore, I have written this book, not in strict editorial fashion, but rather as a relaxed potpourri of sketches and related memories. Each of the countless changes of my life brought a fresh challenge of adjustment, accompanied by the necessary energy flow to match and meet it. The writing of this book was no different.

My abiding interest in the subject of longevity was evidently preprogrammed into my subconscious mind, for I have always been looking out for formulas on non-aging. This is my way of sharing what I have gathered over many years and from many sources. I lovingly hope you will find it useful in your own search to remain forever young.

Sedona, Arizona
September, 1985

CONTENTS

✦FOREVER YOUNG✦

They who can smile when others hate,
Nor blind the heart with frosts of fate —

Their feet will go with laughter bold
The green roads of the never old.

They who can let the spirit shine
And keep the heart a lighted shrine,
Their feet will guide with fire of gold
The green roads of the never old.

◆INTRODUCTION◆

Her initiation began the moment she saw the light of day from a sod-house window on the Cherokee Strip in Oklahoma Territory. Fragments and snatches of her exciting life history, which began some time before the turn of the century, will bear close scrutiny from the reader. From a student at the proverbial little red schoolhouse to an accomplished world traveler and metaphysician, this writer marks a path of trial and error from which we all could learn some lessons.

Things just seemed to happen in her happy, married life that led to a deep appreciation of the universe and the natural laws that make for excellent health and longevity. She combines nutrition and physical fitness with humor and a deep spiritual teaching gleaned from some of the finest minds of the centuries. And it is made to sound so feasible if one will only be observant and adhere to simple rules.

Using the journalistic expertise acquired during her earlier years, she breezes through her lifetime experiences (and visits to 21 countries) with a natural zest that leaves the reader a bit breathless. Her crisp and abbreviated style, with no-nonsense phraseology instantly captures our interest and gives us a yen for emulation.

With astonishing clarity of understanding, the author portrays the teaching of Emanuel Swedenborg, her personal contacts with Yogananda, a love affair with *The Keys of Enoch*, and some other great world teachings. She overviews other subjects, including Tai Chi, Tibetan Yoga, and Rites of Rejuvenation, with diagrammed examples.

Of considerable value is her research and study of nutrition, with many practical hints on how to keep the body in vigorous, healthful condition. Youth is challenged with a few disciplinary hints to the wary. Wrinkles and ineptitude are explained away in personal, therapeutic, and dietary recommendations, which are supported by numerous non-aging techniques. Laughter is the prime tonic.

The esoteric and age-old mystery teachings captured this writer's attention at an early age, and have served as a kind of mirror which she has reflected during her life sojourn. She explains how the older generation must shape up and "get with it" or they will miss the finer forces of nature and a cosmic view of our beautiful universe. She explains that no life is worth living without God's love, a good understanding, and a zest for life — as portrayed in the Qabalah and the Christ cosmic teachings to be found in *The Book of Knowledge: The Keys of Enoch*, which has had a profound influence in her later years.

Past civilizations are also discussed in relationship to possible Earth changes in the near future. Some of these, as diagrammed in the Great Pyramid at Giza, might be achieved through advanced DNA and RNA coding. New magnetic wavelengths now reaching our planet are already having an effect upon human life. Such a potpourri of vital, capsulized information could be extended endlessly and yet never fully satisfy the reader's curiosity and appetite to learn more.

Lehmann Hisey
Sedona, Arizona
October 8, 1985

•1•

YOUTH OUTLOOK

What is youth, after all, but old age without a face. Today we are living in a youth-oriented world which makes maturity and wisdom appear passé. This is not altogether wrong, but it means that the middle-aged and older generations must shape up and refuse to be just tolerated. It seems imperative that they do everything possible to remain young and vibrant, if they are to be accepted.

This classification fits myself, and it gives me great satisfaction to be able to convey the many formulas that I've gathered in stages over the years as a world traveler. The following chapters contain much of what has been discovered in the research on non-aging, as well as what I have learned through personal experimentation and through trial and error.

Let me begin with a brief autobiographical sketch. Long ago, in the late thirties to be precise, I met a remarkable man, Yogananda. Then he was known as a Swami, but after a return to India and a further initiation, he became known as a Paramahansa, or Supreme Soul. He told me of Babaji – head of the hierarchy to which he belonged who, it was said, was thirteen hundred years old. It is recalled that he remarked, "This is only possible by complete dedication to God." This holy man wanted to bring all religions and sects of the world together.

At the time, my youth did not require preservation and my extrovert nature was not seeking a cloistered life. Nevertheless, that such a thing as "longevity" was possible found a niche in my subconscious. Later on, the idea of death seemed absurd and the whole rigmarole of life, with its series of changes — from infancy to youth, coming of age, middle age, or maturity, then declining into old age, and sometimes senility — just did not stack up. If we are supposed to be made in the image of God, then somewhere something went wrong. But what? So began the determination that this "lifestream" would not bow down to what was quoted to be the inevitable: death and taxes. At least not without a struggle to find the answer, somehow, somewhere.

The quest could not have begun in a more appropriate place: the film capital, Hollywood, California, where my spouse was a practicing attorney.

At least, Hollywood was surrounded by freethinkers. And, at the time, yoga exercises and philosophy engaged our attention. Gaylord Hauser's books on diet were enjoying quite a rage. It was from his "potassium cleansing broth" (spinach, celery, parsley), that we partook of our first attempt at good nutrition, along with a series of high colonics.

We spent years in Hollywood, during which great world strides were made: air traffic increased, great highways were built despite the world's longest depression, and numerous innovations came into being. Then the Second World War began, and the Charles Henry Clarks, in their mid-forties, made an early retirement to their ranch where an entirely new life awaited them.

Ordinarily, a quarter of a century's hopes and fulfillment cannot be dismissed in one brief paragraph. Those years were full of activity, work, and play, but also some spiritual realizations. Youth has its strengths, true, but what basis was left upon which to build the other half of our lives?

We could not have adjusted easily to such radical changes had we not been so frightfully busy making smaller changes and trying to improve on nature. Our Hollywood years had been preceded by a year in Portland, Oregon; before that, Chicago; and, some interesting months in the East and North, as well as in the South. We were used to change and found it most stimulating.

At this point in our lives, however, we felt that we needed more of the outdoors. We were both fond of horses and liked to ride. At first, we had a pair of Buckskins, which befitted a raw land background. Sometime later, we acquired a Tennessee Walker with five gaits and, although he was 16 hands high, I enjoyed looking small astride him. Horses were plentiful, with many owners going off to war, so we bought altogether two truckloads of them as we had plenty of pasture land with a stream flowing year-long in the creek.

For two years we became nursemaids to a string of horses, a litter of cats, and a dog or two. Naturally, I was too busy helping to create a livable place from a half-section of raw land to be able to take care of my complexion. And a drastic change from a meat diet to fruits, nuts, and vegetables for six years had left me deficient in the thyroid. Besides, we had a small daughter who required a normal diet. With only one hired hand, we had more work than our pioneering spirit had anticipated.

One special delight which we three looked forward to was visiting Questhaven, an experience which always helped us to maintain a high spiritual level. Questhaven was only four and a half miles as the crow flies, a brisk horseback ride through our neighbor's gates, past Elfin Forest, to Flower Newhouse's Christward Retreat. This was before their beautiful chapel was designed and built. While revisiting recently, I saw that Questhaven had fulfilled all of its early dreams, and that its lovely founder, Flower, is still much in evidence.

After building a wing on the ranch house, mending

fences, planting orchards, and getting five cents-a-pound for lemons, we concluded that despite all the joys of growing our own vegetables, milking a cow, churning butter, and straining clabber for cottage cheese, we were surely going to work ourselves into an early grave. So, we sold out and began traveling.

At first, we took our daughter, Carmelita, with us to the South Sea Islands, Canada, and Mexico. But, she was a poor traveler, and we decided that she would be better off in school, which likewise suited her. Returning from Tahiti, her limbs were red from impetigo, a skin rash which is difficult to control, but which did respond to permanganate of potash.

We thought we had left Hollywood and its glitter and glamour. Nevertheless, it returned to greet us on the Union Steamship Monawai, on its voyage home from the film set of a tropical movie: Douglas Fairbanks, Sr.; William Farnum, of silent movie fame; Eddie Sutherland, the director; and Mary Pickford, at that time Fairbanks' wife, who boarded ship in San Francisco. At this point in my life, I could not help but come in contact with such notables. My most outstanding such memory was the occasion of dining at the table next to Amelia Earhart just a few days before she and her navigator, Fred Noonan, took off on that enigmatic journey. Nine years later, Charles and I had an etheric encounter with her, but more on this later.

My unique background with diametrical changes, perhaps, began at the beginning of my life. Strangely enough, I first saw the light of day from a sod-house window on the Cherokee Strip in Oklahoma Territory, a short time before the turn of the century. My father was a cattle drover and later a range rider, a buffalo hunter, an all-'round wrangler, and a gentleman to boot. He was one of the 60,000 who ran the greatest race for land of all time, and won a quarter section of prairie acres on which, starting from scratch, he built a habitation and raised a family. Briefly, I attended the proverbial little red schoolhouse and, as years passed, I had two years at Normal School before going away to boarding school at Mt. Carmel Academy in Wichita, Kansas.

It was on the train to Kansas City that I met the man of my dreams. Visiting an aunt there turned out to be preparation for a marriage that was to last half a century. This, in capsule form, brings us almost up to date on the idea of keeping young at heart.

We were not a religious family, although I often went to Sunday School with friends, and learned something of Christian doctrine. My father was an agnostic until, on his deathbed, the heavens opened up and he saw his mother who had died when he was a small child. By then, the First World War had come and gone. I had followed my husband to Camp Zachary Taylor in Louisville, Kentucky, and during his officer's training experienced changes that crowded many lifetimes into one.

These events surely made a deep impression on me. More than ever, I wanted to ascertain what life was really all about. I could not forget a most unusual occurrence which took place on the homestead when I was five years old. Two benign men, probably guardian angels if I am to assess them correctly, appeared and talked to me by means of mental telepathy. I recall that even then I could answer them in the same manner, without being in the least afraid. From then on I could feel their presence, and other presences besides. Also I knew that someday I would recall the wonderful ideas they imparted. Although it may seem far-fetched, this does take place...more and more all the time.

•2•

AGELESS SYMBOLOGY

Preventive aging research has brought forth new light which can forestall premature deterioration. Getting away from the Victorian Age and its narrow thinking has been a step in the right direction. Youth, so I have discovered, is a state of mind. Age is not what we think we are; but, what we think, we are. Keep this in mind. Fear is the culprit.

Fear of what? Fear of life; fear of not conforming; fear of a thousand things, probably most important of which is fear of death and what lies beyond that enigmatic journey. Is there really an answer to this mystery? Well, we shall see. Eliminate fear and the battle of life is half conquered.

Without intending to preach or be authoritarian, I can share only what I accept as fact. There is no death. There is only life. Whether in this limited three-dimensional world or in the next, there is no cessation of life. Life is contained in your consciousness. All anybody knows is what is contained in his or her consciousness. Think, stop and think again! Expand your consciousness to include the whole Earth and sky. Keep on expanding it, as the astronomers do, and you can include the galaxies and the super star universe. Life is ad infinitum, always, forever. It can be interrupted only by going into another dimension of space and time.

Meditate on this. As David in Psalms admonished, "Give ear to my words, 0 Lord. Consider my meditation" (Ps. 5:1). Consider first, that in addition to your five outer senses, you possess five spiritual senses — even if they are temporarily atrophied from lack of use. Most of you already know this fact and are restoring the inner senses, which assures you that you are a multidimensional being. Resurrect ye! As the phoenix from its ashes!

Two hundred or more years ago in Sweden, there lived an intellectual and spiritual genius by the name of Emanuel Swedenborg, a nobleman of great stature. Charles and I visited his tomb at Uppsala, where he was buried among the kings. He was a beacon of light after an era of darkness. We first learned about the world beyond from his copious writings; how he was taken in full consciousness to that domain of the Living Dead, the dwellers of which had departed their earthly embodiment. Swedenborg obliquely influenced the New Thought movement — Christian Science, Unity and a dozen or so other minor sects, if they can be categorized as such. Through Swedenborg, numerous early writers and teachers brought forth a grand new outlook to orthodox thinking, much as Martin Luther once did with Protestantism.

The symbols of myth also live on in this way, having long ago departed their earthly embodiment. The present decade, for example, could certainly be described as that of the Unicorn. Everywhere one goes these days, the symbol of the Unicorn is prevalent, etched into greeting cards, appliqued on clothing, printed on calendars. Somehow I feel good about it except that most everyone thinks that the Unicorn is a mythical animal like the Pegasus. It is true that this horse like animal has been extinct for several millennia; but in the time of Job, whose manuscript is the oldest of the Bible (probably a holdover from Atlantis), this graceful animal with a horn protruding from his forehead was an important beast of burden. "Who has put wisdom in the inward parts? Or who hath given understanding to the heart? Will the Unicorn be willing to serve thee, or abide in thy crib? Cans't thou bind the Unicorn with his band in the furrow? Or will he harrow the valleys after thee?" (Job 39:9,10). In Western Canada we once saw a goat-unicorn, as is often depicted in drawings. There he was – a living, breathing Capricornian goat with one horn!

◆3◆

FOLLOWERS OF FALLEN LUMINARIES

It may be true that there is nothing new under the Sun that everything is a replica of something already created in the past. Recently I pondered this trite expression while reading in *The Keys of Enoch*, by Dr. J.J. Hurtak, that the occupants of planet Earth actually had been made in the image and likeness of God, had been given free will, but had chosen to follow fallen luminaries instead. This fouled up the whole God-plan, causing mankind to lose sight of his Light-being. Man grew ever more ponderous as he fell deeper into physicality, until he got trapped in his limited five physical senses, forgetting to use his ethereal sheaths and senses. This sounded logical to me. And, as my childhood mentors suggested, by telepathy I would be able to discern the truth in whatever form it appeared if I persisted.

Persistence is the clue. Once we have decided to reincarnate by our own free will, only we can pull ourselves up, by the grace of God. This requires dedication to Truth, Love, Harmony and Understanding, as Swedenborg pointed out in his writings, as Yogananda suggested, and certainly as has been taught by all the sages and avatars before –

Krishna, Lao-Tzu, Gautama, Jesus, and Zoroaster, to name a few. Is this the mystical reasoning behind our plight? Has humanity used God-energy inappropriately for greed, violence, and dark purposes instead of for supporting light? We do seem to be a wayward planet, going around the Sun like a spaceship with its rudder cut off, oblivious to other worlds that have learned to live in peace and harmony within a federation of space systems. If so, perhaps some day our planet will be able to swing back to its rightful position at the celestial equator and thus eliminate the considerable negativity caused by being out of balance.

How might we overcome our plight? To begin with, we can strive for youth, beauty, and love. Youth is an attitude. It does not succumb to wrinkles or countless birthdays. Indeed, it is best not to think of passing time. A youthful person lives in the now, extracting from life as much as he or she can at each moment. This does not imply that we should plod along in a thoughtless manner, but rather that we must awaken self-discipline, consideration, and compassion for others.

Beauty in all its forms is available to us. With awareness, we can appreciate the tiny details as well as the larger landscapes, and all that they contain of the four kingdoms: the minerals, plants, animals, and people. And, for good measure, let us include the angelic kingdom and all the Hosts of the one Father. Beauty is inside as well as outside. Learning to discover beauty from the inside can be approached not so much by using our eyes, but by feeling it for its own worth. Have you ever noticed how a raving beauty fades by a selfish attempt at sophistication? Or by remarks of envy or jealousy?

Actually, loving everybody is not easy. Nor is it expected of one at first. Nevertheless, we do need to cultivate love. There is no life worth living without it. In fact, love and life are synonymous. Although love of all creation is the goal, one may fall short of this. However, it is hoped that no one will resort to its opposite, hate. Hate-lines in one's face are the ugliest of all. No formula, however expensive, can hide this kind of facial furrow, especially as one grows older.

◆4◆

REJUVENATION
PRACTICES

One good practice is to never go to bed at night without first cleansing the face and applying some kind of skin lubrication. It need not be greasy, just moisturizing. Even while traveling, my last duties were to rinse out our undergarments, nylon for quick drying; then, before jumping in bed, to bathe and apply night cream. Next morning we were ready for a fresh start, usually a city tour, a museum or a flight to some other destination. Although this nighttime routine was sometimes tedious, I never dared to relinquish it.

Our travels usually continued from year to year, sometimes only for a few weeks, but usually for three months or longer. New wardrobes were acquired if we were in an area of favorable currency exchange; and fortunately, from the mid-forties to the eighties, travel was comparatively reasonable.

Having spent some time on the Borrego Desert in California, I always used a cosmetic product called Nivea. It had a moisturizer that helped dry skin and it was reasonably priced. When we were shopping in Madrid, Spain, what did we find but a huge display of Nivea skin care and in greater variety than I ever noticed in the States. At least we were exporting something in exchange for all the shoes and clothes from Spain that filled our shops at home.

It is not really the manufacturer that matters, however. We are inclined to think that if toilet articles are not labeled in France, then they must be inferior. To tell the truth, most face cream formulas are almost identical; perhaps one tiny ingredient may be different but the base is the same.

Body exercise, another good practice, is invaluable for keeping a youthful and agile appearance. I kept up my practice of yoga postures and asanas for several years. In fact, it was after an almost fatal accident, when I did not feel equal to continue these exercises, that my thyroid deficiency ensued. It was not a pleasant situation, but eventually my health improved after the doctor prescribed *Proloyd, a synthetic answer to poor metabolism. In no time, I was a new person and eventually I was able to resume my exercises with Tai Chi, milder in form than my earlier practice of yoga.

Later in life, I came upon a most scientific form of Tibetan Yoga. These remarkable exercises, called The Five Rites of Rejuvenation, are illustrated in the Appendix at the end of this book. Correctly observed, these Rites can stimulate the body's seven vortices, renewing and restoring vital energy to all parts of the body, male or female. Please note that these vortices must not be construed as the eight etheric chakras that overlay the spine – which are also important, especially if one is seeking spiritual advancement.

An additional rejuvenation practice, on which I have done some research, is stimulation of the hypothalamus gland. In ancient times this was referred to as the youth gland. It is a small gland located at the deep cortex of the brain and is the seat of many functions; but, without mental stimulation, it atrophies. The hypothalamus gland is suspected of having been the catalyst which the Sumerian kings' alchemists used for several centuries to preserve the health and vitality of their monarchs. Quite possibly, stimula-

---

This formula was taken off shelves in 1991 for unexplained reasons.

tion of the hypothalamus is the reason why some singers stand on their heads to energize themselves before a performance. At the very least, this posture causes the blood to flow to the tissues of the brain. The whirling dervishes whirl to obtain practically the same effect, only they expect to completely leave their bodies. A combination of the use of crystals and a sunlamp can also stimulate this gland; but if used indiscriminately, this can result in too much absorption at one time and thus may be quite harmful.

•5•

YOUTH IN
AGE-OLD WISDOM

It is possible to live a long life and yet not be living a vibrant, useful life. This is not what is meant in encouraging one to be forever young. As mentioned earlier, youth is a state of mind, but it is also a state of being – more than a frame with a flesh body and a heartbeat inside. It is an awareness that you are a divine creature with unlimited potential. You were thus born with the Tree of Life and the Tree of Knowledge of Good and Evil both within you. Together they comprise the great Tree of Life upon which is to be found the Seven Lustrous Jewels – the shining chakras or spiritual centers.

Although it was not my intention to incorporate the mystery teachings that one usually learns by attending the mystery schools, reference to this age-old wisdom is necessary. I would feel that my duty was not fulfilled if the subject were avoided.

In ancient times, when a child was born, a tree was planted. It was symbolic of the tree associated with the anatomy. We are not a body, per se; we have a body. That is, our body is our animal upon which we ride. Our "I Am presence," our higher self, our Oversoul, whatever term we use, has a three-dimensional body which it uses in the outer world. It is our convenience body and we could not do without it. It also is our Temple and it must be kept holy, for in it our soul-spirit resides for at least as long as we abide in the physical dimension.

From time to time, under varying Rays, there come forth new energies. New books by young authors express fresh revelations of the age-old wisdom in modern languages that may be easier to latch onto by the youth of today. When I was young in spiritual studies, I recall having had a prophecy which stated that, at what was then considered the end of time, there would be a merging of science and religion. I always searched for signs of this cohesion, but only in the last decade, when Dr. J.J. Hurtak wrote *The Keys of Enoch*, did I begin to see any evidence of this prophecy come into existence. Admittedly, science has much knowledge to impart, as does religion; but without an infusion of God, science has no real basis. God Energy, God Life, God Love, God Everything is the source of all. Without it, we would be blotto, nothing. We need to fill ourselves with this divine knowledge and claim our inheritance so that we may be rich in all that we need in this life-dimension and in those to come.

Age-old wisdom revered beauty as a most precious God-given commodity. Have you not met strangers who were almost ugly in appearance until they smiled? After the warmth of such a glowing expression, the space they occupy transforms into a welcoming delight. So it is with the nebulous thing we call love. Love exudes a pink glow. Sometimes it warms as a candle does when lighted in a cold room. Actually, it is a flame, an inner fire glowing for expression. Whoever said that love is what makes the world go 'round certainly expressed a truism; and, not only does love make it go 'round, but smiles make it rebound. I've heard many a tale about what love can do, and personally I've seen it transform by its magical charm.

Beauty is an integral essence of love. These two are

interchangeable. Color is a part of beauty. It is nuclear, or, should we say, atomic. It has a creative and sustaining force. The ancients used color for healing. At Heliopolis, the Greeks constructed healing temples of light and color. The wise old civilizations of India and China glorified healing by color waves and vibrations.

·6·

INNER SHEATHS

B y a strange coincidence, Charles and I found ourselves on a cruise ship in the Aegean Sea in 1957. On the second day out, the Semiramis put into a port known as Kos, the site of Hippocrates' Temple of Medicine, now in Grecian ruins with but a couple of its monolithic columns still standing. In the beginning years of Christianity, this port was known as Coos Bay. This was where St. Paul's prison ship was marooned for months en route to Rome. Here, a viper struck him on the hand and because he did not die the natives thought that he was a god. The healing vibrations are still felt by sensitive visitors to the port. Their fragrance remains, like the indigo blue-green of those enduring waters.

The highly initiated knew the significance of color in relation to the soul and its infinite source. No wonder color often expresses itself in descriptive terms such as "rose-colored spectacles, off color, seen in her true color, green with envy and blue Monday." It is said that Wagner wrote his greatest compositions under the violet light rays filtering through purple curtains. And Leonardo da Vinci, painter par excellence and a great investigator of the science of color, believed that the power of meditation was improved and increased immeasurably by the violet shades of light. When one uses color in certain combinations in decorating or in dress, it gives an elegant effect and lends satisfaction, not only to the viewer but to its creator. I suppose this is why nations and stables design their own color standards.

Words, too, have a hidden power. Longevity is associated with five important words which you should remember. Record them in your mind and refer to them often. They are: I Am, Breath, Light, Love. Actually, a sixth should be added: Laughter. Repeat these simple words often, for they carry more power and permanence than complex instructions ever could.

Let us peek into their significance. "I Am that I Am!" is the answer Moses received when he asked God who he was. Because God is, I Am. Therefore, in His image, I Am. He gave me Breath, Light and Love. I give out my version of these valuable essences and, what is more, they go out on grids of light and on waves of love. And, wherever these ley lines travel, so go my thought forms. Thoughts are things! This has been known and preached by many for several centuries, certainly since Swedenborg's time. Later, this concept was described by Madame Blavatsky, Mary Baker Eddy, Manley Hall, Ernest Holmes and others such as Max Heindel and Rudolf Steiner.

When analyzing ourselves, to omit the fact that we have spiritual senses, subtle sheaths, together with our five physical senses would be incomplete. How else would we ever be conscious in the higher dimensions? God does not do things halfway, to be sure. Yes, we are most complex and highly organized, if we only knew it. As a matter of fact, each one of us is unique, one of a kind, yet we all share the same divine origin. Just think of that!

.7.

LONGEVITY BEGINS WITH
GOD AWARENESS

When I was a youngster, I often heard people remark, "What is a body to do?" This just goes to show how ignorant we were then, but how about now? Can you think of yourself somewhere in your higher self with your higher faculties, as cosmic laws allow?

Only one of our sheaths left the ivory palaces to come down to the three-dimensional physical world. The higher part of us is still there, too pure and too wise to have ventured out. Now, we can still hook up with that glorious part of ourselves that the sub- or unconscious part of ourselves craves to know. Yes, it is so. To know it is amazing. It opens up an entirely new love affair with God and yourself, a relationship which bestows confidence, assurance, and permanence. Once security is established, no longer do you fear anything or anybody because you have a handle on divinity and God is your source, comfort, and strength. His power and His presence ride along with you wherever you go. You are never alone. This knowledge is only the beginning fact of longevity, for with it comes rejuvenation and restoration for a completely new self.

How shall we care for this sheath which entered the

physical world? Shall we disdain or deny it, as some sects
teach? `Actually, *The Book of Knowledge* infers that we
should lighten up our bodies in two ways; eat fewer gross
foods and more foods of a high vibratory nature, and also
lighten your weight to what is normal for your frame. Fresh
fish is a commonsense food, much easier on the digestive
juices than is red meat, which is digested much more slowly.
Besides, these slaughtered animals share the same right to
life that we do and this planet belongs as much to them as it
does to us, even though they are on a lower evolutionary
scale than we are.

In the strictest sense, I am not a true vegetarian. For
my needs, I try to be moderate in all things. I prefer nuts,
grains, and seeds to meat and I feel less like a cannibal when
eating them. Recently the turkey products, such as turkey
ham, turkey pastrami, and turkey sausage and frankfurter,
have occasionally been acceptable and palatable for my diet.
My holistic doctor tells me that dairy products should be
avoided; and although I am cutting down on them, I am not
ready to dispense with them entirely. I take some calcium
supplements, some with bone meal and another with oyster
shells ground to powder. Gaylord Hauser claimed that our
bodies need portions of the 16 minerals that we were born
with and if these are not supplied our resistance to disease
diminishes. As this seems logical, I have tried without making a fetish of food, to follow his conclusion in my diet. Of
course, vitamins are important – C, E and A are must.
Sometimes B6, B12 and bee and flower products are added;
and at other times, supplements such as spirulina and gold-
enseal are included. As with so many other things, I will
often try out a supplement for a while and then abandon it
for a trial of something else. The same goes for toilet articles; I've tested all kinds.

The one thing that is necessary for my diet is fruit,
especially apples the year 'round. When seasonal fruits are
fresh, I usually gorge myself on them: peaches, plums, pears,

apricots, strawberries and almonds. We usually think of almonds as nuts, but the first time I was in France I learned otherwise. There, immature almonds were sold in their peachlike shells and on sprigs, just like peaches. I tried out these soft kernels and liked them so much that we planted almond trees at the ranch. Nothing is more beautiful than an almond tree in bloom. With its thick, snow-white blossoms in January (in California), it looks like something the snow fairy would produce. Beautiful to gaze upon!

•8•

REVELATION OF REBIRTH

I had not yet arrived at the point where signs of old age overtook me, partly because I was unaware of the ravages of time. My dressing room at Del Mar, California where we lived for 14 years between trips, had a northern exposure and my stealthy wrinkles went largely unnoticed until it was almost too late. Charles, if he did notice them, accepted them as normal. At least he did not attempt to smooth them out. Charles looked the same to me, as well, although he had thickened around the midriff and his once dark, wavy hair had grown thin. Neither of us had grayed very fast. Other things occupied our attention and we had each other. Did anything else matter?

Yes, we had our arguments for neither of us demanded the other to believe the same way. Freedom of thought was a priceless privilege. This was how we learned, but we did do a lot of sharing. In spite of arguments, we shared an appreciation for each other's unique gifts and talents, some indigenous to our nature, others acquired by study and training. Charles was the scholar, whereas I — in my intuitive fashion — absorbed by osmosis. We each came to believe in the doctrine of rebirth or reincarnation, although we arrived at it by different methods.

This knowledge was first revealed to me before I was acquainted with the word for it. In a vision, while under ether for minor surgery, I experienced important portions of several lifetimes, so real that they were relived momentarily. In two lives I had similar spouses and these were most harmonious. However, as the anguish of parting with each one faded, I started through a tunnel in which a man approached from the other end. As he came closer, I recognized him and turned back, saying, "Not you again!" Then the wise one by my side, known only by his voice, cautioned me, "Don't be too hasty. In this lifetime you have a chance to make amends." Suddenly I had a flash of tragedy almost too sad to bear; it was about an event that had happened in remote ages. And I was able to heed the admonition of this wise voice, for he enumerated the loyalty and ability and love of this man who just happened to be my husband of 13 years at that time.

This experience sobered me. My soul responded immediately to its verity and, although the knowledge dimmed in time, its spark never went out. It sealed my determination to make amends in the best way that I could. Fate brought us together and kept us together through thick and thin.

Charles must have been convinced of rebirth through reading. I had told him about my vision, but not until four years before his demise did he ever acknowledge that we knew each other in Greece centuries before. After a pacemaker installation, his doctor awakened him, asking, "Where were you? I thought you were going to sleep all day." Whereupon Charles answered, "I was in Greece, wearing a sissy uniform of antiquity, more feminine than we wear today." There it was!

.9.

COPING WITH REALITIES

M any questions have been asked of me concerning non-aging. I reply, "What worked for me may not necessarily work for you, but it is for you to store in your subconscious or unconscious mind and to draw from when you need it."

After radio interviews, the station usually gets a few telephone calls from listeners wishing to pursue a topic of special interest. Questions about skin care I answer without hesitation. More personal questions, like how to cope with living alone after having had a companion for 50 years, I do not answer. No one having had the exciting life that Charles and I lived together, exploring continents in search of answers to their antiquity and related cultures, can ever cope with the loneliness of those spare moments of not being engaged in some task or project. If I were not busy, busy, busy most of every waking hour, it would be just too difficult. Yet, one is never alone. Charles is ever with me in my thoughts of gratitude to him and to God, as my unseen guides reveal when I take time to listen.

Once I was asked by a younger man who had known me earlier, "Are you still here? What is your secret for re-

maining active for so long?" To his amusing inquiry I had
an amusing answer: "I laugh a lot. I look for the funny
things in life instead of the sordid."

Just recently I took a friend's granddaughter to obtain
a "reading" from a middle-aged friend of mine who is multi-
talented in music as well as iridology, hypnotherapy, and
several other "ologies." I am sure that from the hour with
him she will begin a new life program. Not only was this
darling teenager partly deaf from child abuse, but a special
fate directed her to many new fields of endeavor after her
exposure to an alcoholic environment. Her interview was
taped so that it could be heard time and again, if needed, yet
this dear one has the most unique sense of humor and re-
sponse. She recalls these lessons as only stepping stones,
and sees nothing but a bright future of her own making.
This is what laughter can do. We laughed at these former
impediments, obliquely knowing that, with the certainty of
God's grace and unction, everything is and will be in divine
right order. This knowledge stimulated an inner merriment.
Laughter is from within. It can be faked, but not convinc-
ingly.

I have a friend of long standing who writes to me frequently. In every letter, she encloses some amusing anec-
dote or a comic strip, and never falls to mention that my
letters bring inspiration to her. Formerly, she had been a big
game hunter with her sportsman spouse. Later, she recalled
that she couldn't bear the luxury of the "game room," with
those glassy eyes of the stuffed animals looking accusingly
at her. Eventually she vacated the house, allowing her
spouse to keep the inanimate specimens of wildlife. Once
they were snowbound in Alaska for six months, an ideal
opportunity for her to do a lot of sane thinking. It was then
that she realized that, although she was an expert with a
rifle — a "sure-shot" — her prowess became past tense.

◆10◆

LONGEVITY IN JAPANESE ROYAL QUARTERS

One of my most priceless foreign collections is an antique saki jar. It was presented to me by a prince in Tokyo. Our relationship started in 1929 on our first voyage to Europe. Charles and I met him and we all became friends aboard the "SS Albertic" of the Cunard Line. Later, we met again in Trafalgar Square in London and decided to take the train to Yorkshire to visit mutual friends there. We had no idea, then, of his ancestry or rank. John, as we called him, was charming and sad at the same time. He was in love with an American girl but sorrowful that he could not marry her impulsively, like we do in this country of freedom. After graduating from Harvard, he was on his way home by stages. While we were admiring our host's collection of ivory, John remarked that his father also had such a collection and that their family had entertained General Pershing of World War I fame. This should have given us a clue, but young people are more apt to like or dislike others, never giving a thought to origin. As far as I was concerned, I kept my sod-house origin a deep, dark secret.

Later, we met John in Paris and went night clubbing at

the Montmartre and scavenging elsewhere, for we were
young and craved excitement. At 2:00 a.m. Charles and I
rose to depart, as we were returning to California the next
day. John preferred to remain, but next morning appeared at
our hotel door and laughingly reported in his charming English, "I was rolled."

"What are you going to do?" we asked.

"Well, I've already been to the Japanese Embassy, and
they will fix me up," he said, using American slang.

It was not yet 8:00 on a Sunday morning, and we mentioned the absurdity. "And we suppose you woke up the
ambassador himself to get you out of your fix?"

"Right, and that is what they are for!"

It was a reluctant parting, but each of us had packing
to do. That was the last time we met for 30 long years.

Meanwhile, the war had ended, the war in which the
U.S. and Japan engaged in hostilities. We wondered what
fate John had experienced. Then, while in Australia, we decided to return home via the Orient. Our pilot on Quantas
reminded the passengers that we had just passed the Inter-
national Date Line and that we were arriving a day earlier
than our hotel reservations might be for, and he recommended three Japanese hotels for the night. We chose the
Di Itshe, which he advised that Japanese liked. Next morning when we paid our bill, Charles asked the English-speak-
ing clerk what I thought was a perfectly inane question.
Here we were in the largest city in the world at that time,
having had no word from John for three decades; yet, Charles asked if the clerk had any idea where we could find John
Sago. Of course, he did not. But I said, "He graduated from
Harvard in 1929 and played on the tennis team."

"Aha! Yes, I know him. But that is only his pseudonym.
His company owns this hotel." And he proceeded to get
John on the telephone so that we could set up an appoint-
ment with him for the next day.

John looked more mature, of course. He readily recognized Charles and me. En route to his estate, John wheeled us by the Imperial Palace, making more reference to the landscaping than to the architecture. At his home we were shown which part of his menage was English and which part pleased his lovely wife, who had not yet made an appearance. He had sired seven children, two of whom were in Eastern colleges. Asota soon entered, looking like a schoolgirl herself and wearing the kimona of the old order, with the full obi tie at the back waist. I commented on how young she looked, and John interpreted her answer: "She says that she never worries, but leaves all the important decisions to me." What a revelation and what a valuable tip for Americans to adopt, I thought.

Before we left, pictures were taken to compare with our former pictures taken together in England. Then John pointed to some vases on the English mantle, asking, "Do you like them?"

Naturally, I said, "Oh, they are beautiful. I always have admired those with the fine cracks in the porcelain."

"Gladys*, you have passed the test. Satsuma Ware is one of our priceless heritages, and Asota wants to present you with an antique specimen. The emperor gave the vases to my father, his brother, long ago and we have great appreciation for them."

The gift, all tied with a fiber ribbon, was contained in beautiful wooden box, which I now use for a receptacle next to my dressing table. The vase, or jar, has an antique shade of pale brown, in which the subtle Oriental design appears from the depth of the glaze in subdued jade and saffron colors. An exquisite object to behold.

"Please tell us how you fared during the war," Charles asked.

"I was thought by the war consul to be pro-American, so my estate was confiscated and I was put to work driving a

---

Gladys is name used then, but Iris is name frequently used today.

lorry most of the time. Our grounds were strafed and my mother's cottage on the estate was bombed by Doolittle's Tokyo air raid, but fortunately she was in our house at the time. Later, when General McArthur presided over the reparations of our nation, my estate was restored to us. In the exchange, Tokyo was given a new city park."

In this encounter with Japanese royalty, I learned a tiny bit of their secret for staying young. The women, for the most part, let their men folk do all the worrying about outside affairs, and they engage only in the domestic affairs concerning childbearing and childrearing. This arrangement seems to add to their initial charm, like a glow from live coals.

◆11◆

MYSTERIOUS ENIGMAS

After our escape from ranch drudgery and while reasonably young, we toured Mexico and Central America. But we had not yet touched foot on South American soil. Charles was specifically interested in what he had read about Colonel Faucet's fatal explorations near the Amazon, but I was adamant about not letting Charles end up in any cannibal stew. We agreed, therefore, to keep very much to the civilized parts.

Our main problem was getting passage on a steamship which was not already booked full, due to the shortage of vessels in 1946, just after the war. From Phoenix, Arizona, we drove our newly acquired Mercury station wagon, which had been issued to us by permit in exchange for a DeSoto, no longer in production. We felt very lucky to get one of the first domestic cars off the assembly line after several war years. The Delta Line put our names on the waiting list for passage to Rio de Janeiro, via Haiti and Martinique – scene of a devastating earthquake in Pele around the turn of the century, and also where the Empress Josephine, Napoleon's wife, was born a century or more before. All this was awaiting us in New Orleans if only the new ship Del Norte could get commissioned, return from her shakedown cruise, and sail on her maiden voyage. It would be well worth the long weeks of waiting.

To kill time, we drove to Miami, Florida. En route, along Highway 90 near the little town of Bonifay, we looked up. Overhead we saw lights approaching us like an oncoming freight train, and glowing red like an engine afire. Lower and lower in the sky it traveled, until we heard a tremendous blast in the air. We later learned that it was a red fireball. It must have been an atmospheric explosion that sounded as it reached our atmosphere. I expected atomic particles to fall in our path, but none did, for the fireball zoomed over some swamp trees to the left of the highway, and in a twinkle was out of sight. We were so full of shock that we could not go on, although it was only 8:00 p.m. Next morning a hurricane was brewing in the Atlantic and threatening the southern seaboard. With all attention geared to protecting lives and property against the storm, I found it difficult to explain what we had seen to the reporter of the Tallahassee *Democrat*.

This was the only time we ever attempted to report a UFO, although we had already seen two different types of this still-mysterious enigma. The huge mother ships we saw one July night, while sleeping under the stars in California's Borrego Desert, have been identified and categorized since 1946, at least to our satisfaction. Recently, in the study of *The Keys of Enoch*, I learned that such space vessels of the higher type are referred to as biosatellites, or Merkabah.

That November of 1946, I was witness to other incredible materializations. From Miami we went on to Coral Gables, where we attended a seance by a noted spiritual medium named Berty Lily Candler, whose materializations were heralded all through the South. Earlier awarded a Eugene Field certification and a membership in the National Journalistic Society, I was eager to ply my talents, if any. What we witnessed that night was so awe inspiring that it changed my entire metaphysical outlook, causing me to wonder whether I had spent years studying the subject to vain conclusions. This middle-aged, chubby woman allowed me to inspect her cabinet, which consisted only of corner drapes in a block building structure, a couch, and a tiny Pomeranian dog. Berty Lily Candler was the only addition, dressed in a flimsy kimono, a pair of shorts, and no bra.

First a small, childlike spirit was heard to announce that the medium was now in trance. Then suddenly a hearty Indian chief in full regalia bounded forth in a familiar dance, his voice booming in rhythm with his hooplas. I could almost see the dust rise from the floorboards as he jumped around in authentic Red Man's traditions (being from the Oklahoma Territory, I had watched their dances time and again). After his sudden departure, who should confront us but the long lost female flier, Amelia Earhart! She was authentic, if ever a spirit could be – a tall, graceful figure as big as life and momentarily, at least, breathing and functioning as a person, as she talked to a couple who moved up to the low stage rostrum to communicate with her. She had that same washed glow to her skin, never powder or makeup; her natural, wavy hair was windblown and cut short, the same as ever. We wanted to be allowed to speak to her, but were under rules not to disobey procedure. Anyway, I was glued to my chair and doubt if I could have moved. The ivory satin frock she wore draped in folds over her lean, lanky frame. Gad, what happened?

After this, came a dozen or more materializations of the audience's loved ones, including Charles' mother, whose demise had occurred two decades earlier. My thoughts, however, were on Amelia and the dramatics of seeing her in her etheric reality when all the world wanted to know the details of her tragedy. What a literary scoop it would have been, if I had only had the ability to comprehend the modus operandi of translation from one dimension into a higher frequency. I swore to myself then and there that I would never stop seeking answers to our multi-dimensional selves.

What if the yogins were right in claiming that we live as if in a dream and that we wake up in reality after the physical shell is discarded?

As soon as the seance was over, I hastened to interview the couple that greeted Amelia. They said that they had not known her in person, but that she had made several appearances there, looking so lonely and casting glances around. They wished to put her at ease and welcome her. According to their report, Miss Earhart was trying vainly to contact her mother and sister in New England to let them know that she was still in charge, albeit in a realistic world where ambition does not overrule.

"Tell me," I inquired with strong fervor, "do you know what happened?" We urged as if life and death hung in the balance, and I guess it once did. "Tell us what went wrong, if you know!"

"Yes, we will reveal all that we found out when we asked her that same question." Amelia said, "I overshot the mark."

"Did she say if anything else happened to her?" I asked. "Were any of the rumors true that she had been a government spy and that the Japanese took her captive?"

"Yes, we even asked her about that, but she answered placidly, 'There were some complications, but that is all over now and it certainly has no importance now. Let it go. Don't you see that I am all right now?' "

Strangely enough, I never felt qualified to write up this factual story of Amelia's fate taken from her own etheric lips, until this very moment. In my 98th year, I concluded that if I were ever to tell it at all, it had best told now or never. There you have it! Ponder it wise asking yourself if, when the time comes, you are willing to escape the spectre called death and keep on living harmonious life in the spirit. If so, you have nothing fear. As the song goes, "There is only one Power."

◆12◆

OTHER SLANTS

About materializations, McDonald Baines, who spent years in the temples of Tibet, exchanging ideas with the lamas, wrote in *The Yoga of The Christ*, "Oh infinite one, thou dost water the yielding crops that grow without man's aid. All that was to plant the seed and thou didst mold the earth and sprinkle it with sun and rain. We will all live joyfully in the Cosmic Temple of the living God, to the glory of the Father and brotherhood of mankind."

St. Anthony said, "There is only one substance out of which everything is made (created). This one substance underlies all forms, all manifestation, though in different degrees. You are functioning in and through them all, though you are not aware of them. At present you are uniting in the material, but that is merely a modification of the one substance. It is a degree and not separate."

From time to time, I make notes in order to reread them for inspiration. Unfortunately, they are made carelessly, without signifying the author. I hope that the author of the following note considers it a compliment instead of a plagiarism to be quoted: "The willows whisper, 'On the many branches of my Tree of Life I have sung my song of love. As

my song was echoed in the green leaves, those who heard
me realized their oneness with me. Then my life alone was
food for them. All through the centuries of time my timeless state remains. That is why sleeping souls in the world
of time can still waken unto me. The rhythm of my song
stirs the hearts awaiting to hear my voice calling: So we
must arise and go.'" Watch the mind when it stops fabricat-
ing. This is true meditation. Listen for your song of love,
in quiet repose.

Ultimately, the subject of materializations raises the
question of chemistry. What is the substance of the higher
forms of UFO? St. Anthony offers an answer in the above
quote. Some call it Foat, some Aeth, the Hindus call it
Prana, and the Indians have their own name for it. We call it
the breath and substance of life. Teilhard de Chardin said,
"Someday after we have mastered the winds and the waves
and tides and gravity we shall harness for God the energies
of love. Then for the second time in the history of the
world, man will have discovered fire." We have all heard of
love as a consuming flame. Love is the light of life. Without
it we are dead already, but do not know it.

Omni magazine writers admit to four dimensions, and
one writer thinks that there are at least 11. Actually, there
are 24 dimensions, if you want to get way out in the super-
universe. Out where the biosatellites roam.

·13·

NON-AGING TECHNIQUES
IN ACTION

As I have compiled and developed my own research and relations on non-aging, I have been heartened to learn that others have begun to think along similar cosmic lines. At least one Think Tank is devoted exclusively to the last third of life. Perhaps they won't mind if mention is made of the principles which they embrace:

The Last Third of Life Club founded by Jerome Ellison

One: We admit that death is closer for us who are in the last third of our lives than it is for the average person; that in this respect we are different from the majority of people.

Two: We have come to see that, for those who are prepared, the eventual passage from this life can be a glory rather than a dread.

Three: We have decided to use our remaining years primarily for this preparation.

Four: We assert that the last third of life is given by nature for this high purpose; that it can illuminate all earlier experience in the joyous fulfillment of a rounded life.

Five: We have resolved to give over our lives to Cosmic Creative Intelligence as we individually name and experience this divine force.

Six: Through regular morning and evening meditations, we are finding ourselves more and more in harmony with this transcendent power.

Seven: Reviewing our past in the company of other Last Thirders has shown us that our earlier life goals no longer suffice.

Eight: Through reading, discussion, and reflection we have humbly attempted to discover and cultivate those higher values that are essential to our new life.

Nine: Having thus gained a clearer perspective on life's major-phases, we have steadfastly sought the wisdom it is the business of life's later years to acquire and preserve.

Ten: These steps have brought an awareness of cosmic dimensions we had not hitherto explored and have led us into the realm of deep spiritual experience.

Eleven: Though aware that the workday world undervalues spiritual wisdom, we offer what we have of it when asked.

Twelve: As our special responsibility, and as opportunity offers, we carry to others in the final third of life the heartening word that seniority can be joyous.

•14•

MUSING ON TRANSITION

Written January, 1977, the night of Charles Henry Clark's departure.

Epitaph to a Departing Paraclete

The mantle of flesh was not myself,
Tho' from it my immortal soul tore –
To enter its newly found freedom.
In my ethereal garment I'm more alive
Than ever before. [In ages past my
Spirit lived a thousand times or more].
The seed atoms contained all the soul's
Essence in a celestial computer to store.
Memories still haunt me of the diverse
Lives I've lived; of dissimilar tongues
My lips have spoken. In each incarnation
Some talents were acquired [most to my
Credit but many verboten]. Between
Times great changes transpired – to these
My restless soul made difficult adjustments,
As divine law required.
To explain the purpose of the grand

Scheme of things: Repetition of lives
Allows my identical spirit continuity
To express itself in ways that bring
A complete cycle of zodiacal swings—
Until at last in a body of LIGHT
I'm weighed on a celestial scale.
Triumphant, like a god with all
Banners unfurled, I enter Zion's
Golden Gate as a perennial scholar
To learn the uses of sacred Energy.
There it is my choice to remain
To beam healing rays to earthbound
Mortals. Or, if I desire to tread
The earth once more, in brotherly
Love, I shall "set sail."

Death, as we are wont to think of it and as it is gener-
ally accepted, appears to be the final dissolution of the body.
This kind of death is believed to be not heroic but final. I
know differently. While it is not easy to focus in on my
dearly departed's transition, to exclude such experience
would alter and cut the thread of the whole theme on which
this book is based: Life! Immortal life, continuous, ever
active, ever creative.

Earthborn man is in the learning process and is given a
field on which to play and work out his experiments. What
is learned is stored in the soul's computer. When one knows
this, death has no sting. But when first confronted with the
evidence, how does one react? Will one's philosophy of life
hold fast? In my case, it did.

After three years with a pacemaker, to which Charles
could not reconcile himself — neither to its rhythm nor to its
necessity — he left the dust world for life in the more subtle
crystalline realms. It had been his time three years before
and he knew it, though I did not. Had he not been captive
to medical authority, and to my persuasion, he would have

been spared the indignity and trauma of a cerebral hemorrhage later. Although we did consequently have three more years together, the end was rugged instead of the tranquil way he would probably have slipped out of his body when the silver cord was ready to rent.

In Ecclesiastes we read that there is a time for everything: a time to be born, a time to die.... But are we wise enough to bow to this divine decision, unselfish enough to let our loved ones depart in peace? It is my hope in relating this episode that more people will have the strength and moral courage to defy the hierarchy of the hospitals when occasion demands.

In increasing numbers of states, it is now legal to have a living will. Basically, a living will is a written statement by a person, which documents that he or she does not wish to be kept alive artificially under stated circumstances. This legislation gives adults the fundamental right to control decisions relating to their own medical care, including withholding special measures taken to prolong life. Such options did not exist when Charles and I had to face the medical practitioners following his hemorrhage.

All during this period of caring for him, I was sustained by energy from on high; and for the most part, I thought of it as a loving chore to the end. No, I did not grieve for him. I knew that he knew and that he longed to be released from his flesh vehicle, which no longer functioned normally. And yes, simply because one learns to depend on another, I grieved for myself. Now I was on my own and no longer would I have a most desirable escort and travel companion to arrange all sorts of fascinating trips and places to go.

When do the so-called dead become alive again? According to Swedenborg, it varies according to the entity's awareness. He writes that the most advanced souls often go directly into the Father's House, and that no one leaves Earth without an escort. Among the myriad of angels in various spheres, the highest are the angels of birth and death. I am forever thankful that, after several months of Charles' demise, he appeared to me in full complement to his younger self. He appeared at his highest mental maturity, around 35, perhaps. I saw him coming down a long slope before me, smiling as usual and wearing a trim gray suit as of yore. As he approached, I asked: "How did you know where to find me?" In typical legal fashion, he answered: "Well, we have ways and means to do that." I caught up with him and started to walk beside him, when suddenly he was no longer visible.

This visitation came rather early one morning when I was sitting on the sofa in the living room. I cherish this indelible picture, for it confirms to me that in his ethereal garment he was a whole man, not one confined to a wheelchair. His ascension was complete. And I know that he wanted to show me this fact.

15

WISDOM
OF THE AGES

In the hall of learning, which is another name for the Kingly Ruler within your heart – where spirit is permitted to flow unaided and unshackled in a consciousness pure enough to allow it, the One Presence exists beyond time and space. This is poetically called, by the ancient Chinese, "The Yellow Castle of the Space of Former Heaven." In this purple heart of the City of Jade, we are given a comparative description of the City Foursquare as revealed by St. John the Divine. "In the field of the square inch[1] of the house of the square foot[2] dwells the Splendor," says an Oriental sage, "where one hears the flutes of angels."

Listening to this Song of Life, one hears speech. Silently through your own heart comes the one Light which illuminates Life and makes it clear and concise. Relative things vanish, for these turn to ashes like the Dead Sea fruit in the light of the permanence of the One Reality. It is said that when this fount is opened and the Elixir of Life is partaken of, then shall there be no more thirst. In the Sun's soft light, in the witchery of night, in the stone and in the flower, every object of nature is the song of harmony with

---

[1]*The third eye.*   [2]*The face*

the same chant that it heard on the farthest star. This voice of spirit beats upon the ears. Listening to the lilt of the grand volume as it reaches a high crescendo, one hears it whispering, "Be faithful in learning the mystery that surrounds you, until every veil is rent."

The eye that sees and knows all is the Akashic Records. Did you know that everything you think, say, feel and do is recorded? Forever recorded in such a way that anyone who knows how to clairvoyantly unscramble the record can reproduce it again, as clearly as a voice on the telephone or as plainly as transcribed on a radio program or as pictorially as film is unreeled on a picture screen. Even your feelings and voice are recorded. There are no secrets, for the seeing Eye of Horus knows all. As Shakespeare said in *Hamlet*, "There are more things in heaven and earth, Horatio, than are dreamt of in your philosophy." Trite, but nevertheless, true as rain.

The Great Principle Science of the Soul, by Lyctu advises: "Learn to be cheerful, equable, poised. Get rid of old restraints, superstitions, fetishes. But go gently. Don't use violence on your soul. Don't hide your weaknesses from yourself, but don't exaggerate them either. Take nothing too seriously, yourself least of all. Live each day as though it were to be your last, without superimposing your will on anyone or without the will others superimposed on you." A cheap philosophy, but good for the soul and nerves!

⋆16⋆

CANCEL OUT
NEGATIVES

This is a chapter that I dislike having to write. It is about obesity and smoking. These subjects have little in common, but they come under the classification of negative subjects. Obesity has always stalked me around the corner, but I am a formidable foe and I try to hone my sword sharply enough to strike it down before complacency gets the best of me. If we do not take dominion over the appetite, then these little elementals will take dominion over us. Do not imagine that they are not intelligent. They know when we are most vulnerable, and this is when they set up those hunger pains. It is as if they are saying, "You are starving our cells. We want you to swill us. We like to hog it. Our molecules need fat! How about eating what's left of that pie?" Well, do not believe them! Enough is enough! Like all negatives, they can be overpowered by reason and right action.

This approach will also help to curb smoking. When we smoke, we let our nerves, instead of our cells, dictate our behavior. My darling relative claims that a cigarette calms her nerves; that it is central to her concentration in spatial thinking; and that, since one has to die of some cause, are not cigarettes more satisfactory than other habits like gossiping and criticizing others? Subconsciously, a smoker knows that the weed (ages ago, cigarettes were referred to as weeds; now we use the term to indicate marijuana and other grasses) is, as TV ads claim, injurious to one's health. Perhaps antismoking ads could be more successful with a new tack, such as "Want to be captain of yourself? Be totally free! Are you smart enough to say no to an inanimate habit, or must you admit that you are self-enslaved?" We fight determinedly to see that all nations and peoples are free from oppression, and yet we submit to personal habits that can cause untold damage to the organ that gives us breath — the lungs. Habits like overeating and smoking are inane indulgences that should be opposed just as one would avoid jumping off a cliff. Self-discipline is critical to longevity. Although I may not succeed, at 98 years of age, I am still trying.

·17·

GRECIAN NOSTALGIA

A nd what about our social habits?   Are we really behaving like members of an advanced civilization? Considering that in ancient times, Charles and I lived in Greece, it was only natural for us to make three excursions back to what was once our homeland – not to tour, but to really come to know the place. On our first voyage, we were unable to find accommodations in Athens because of a wine festival being held there. So we quite by accident, found ourselves cruising on the Aegean Sea. One of the islands we visited was Delos, an ancient seat of culture.   French archaeologists were on the spot at the time. We visited their digs and were particularly impressed with the mosaic tile art – on floors, walls, and benches as well.   One wall scene depicted a tiger on the prowl. The artist had taken pains to use infinitesimal tiles for eyelashes, making his eyes so realistic!   As in several other ancient digs, chiseled lions formed a guard a quarter-mile long facing the sea. Everywhere we went, we found the remnants of copper objects, some just lying on the ground.

On our second trip to Greece, we took quarters at a new hotel in Amonio Square, near the entrance to a subway.

One day, we rode the subway to the outlying town of Mon-
striki, where artifacts were lying about on the ground in an
ancient cemetery. A large, sculptured bull still stood near
the entrance which, to me, signified that it had remained
there since the age of Taurus. Bulls were also depicted on the
island of Crete. I had been impressed while living in the ranch
house and reading about the antiquities of Crete, but never did
I imagine that tramping over the same earth as the Spartans
had centuries earlier would give me an eerie feeling. Truly, it
almost transported me back to the distant time when Spartans
sought perfection in their lives and culture.

Sparta was the most barren and rugged of the whole
Peloponnisos. Sparta! No wonder the derivation of the
word "spartan." Their economy was so frugal that the people were not allowed to let deformed babies live. They threw
them over the cliffs. But they did — like every other age and
nation — sacrifice their sons, during the flower of their
youth, in needless wars.

We call ourselves civilized, but where, over the ages on
our planet, have we not waged wars? I have found, for example, that my four major family-line ancestors fought in the
Revolutionary War. In fact, I have had family members in
every war since our country's inception, except for the Span-
ish-American War. Come to think of it, none of our sons
served in the Korean or Vietnam wars; but then, neither
were these wars declared.

Until we can settle our disputes amicably, we will still
be a barbaric planet, a sort of reform school where, in this
particular universe, they send the incorrigibles. It is a beautiful Earth, but what a travesty we have made of it. No
wonder the knowledgeable Earth retaliates and periodically
shakes loose its pollution and corruption. Geologists have
determined, by observing the twisted rock strata, that axial
shifts have occurred many times in the past. And seismologists,
even on TV, report that reversal of the poles is long past due.

◆18◆

EARLY
PROPHECIES

S t. Hildegarde, an astounding original thinker of the dark
ages, believed that war is not so much a destruction of
life as it is a waste of forms. According to her thought, you may
starve and beat a man, you may burn or bind him, you may
torture him on the rack, but this will only make the body suffer.
One cannot hurt the soul. She asked for a vision, and it was
given to her. She was shown that in distant eras, during such
times of human violence, destruction would greatly increase
upon the Earth. All the evils of the known world's then-small
area were greatly increased. Entire continents would fight each
other, for only through this process could the human belief in
the significance and divinity of the body break down.

To this day, man continues to regard the body with
peculiar affection. His first thought is to comfort it. He is
more interested in his possessions and material comforts
than in his spiritual development. Man is most miserable
when his body hurts, most happy when his body is advanta-
geously placed; most proud when his body is honored, and
most abject when his body has been dishonored.

St. Hildegarde made some predictions that have already
come about. Most notably, she believed that war evils will con-

tinue until man naturally reforms and all men become mys-
tics, because mysticism by its very nature is the antithesis of
war.[1]

Let us look at what the prophecies of just a decade ago
have to say. Hurtak was taken up by Enoch and, after fasting
and seeking answers, he was shown the blueprint for humanity
and the planet we occupy. At long last, when we have lifted
ourselves up out of the gravitational field into the levitational
field, the planet is destined to take its place in the Federation of
the Universe. This is rapidly coming about at the present time.
For the first time in history, sufficient numbers of enlightened
men and women exist to cause this to happen. The Ascended
Ones and the more lofty space beings, along with the Christed
Hierarchy, are using the One Power and Presence of the I Am
motivation to bring this to pass. The fallen ones that have held
sway over this planet, whose false teachings have kept us
chained in a third-dimensional bind for these many millennia,
are being forced back out of our planetary environment. And
the Cosmic Christ is moving in to take charge, with the prayers
and invocations of the Earth luminaries.

When the moment arrives, a gradual turnover will take
place. This is when the separating of the sheep and the goats
will occur. Those unable (or whose body systems are too
coarse) to withstand the high frequencies will be taken away to
where they can function, but the elect will be spirited away on
one of the biosatellites and endued with its wisdom.

Years ago, when I was attracted to the inner wisdom,
the standing prophecy was that at the End Time, orthodox
religion would be supplanted by a union of science, religion
and government. This would gradually emerge as a solution
to the world's problems, reported the prophecy. Perhaps
government, with its fear of a state religion, is not yet ready.
But I daresay that when the representatives in government
become Christed, such a merging could be possible.

---

[1]*This material has been condensed from Horizons andcompiled from the voluminous
writings of Manley Palmer Hall.*

◆19◆

POSSIBLE
EARTH CHANGES

The time is approaching when religion will become scientific. It is already gradually taking place and must, at any rate, come to fruition before the next major Earth Change. We are trusting that these Changes will not be as violent and devastating as the current negative predictions would have it. At this foretime, the Earth inhabitants will hopefully be enlightened enough to stay the effects of a world cataclysm. The decades of the fifties and sixties marked the time for answering the call of preparation. By becoming focused on the lofty state of consciousness, the personal revelation will be able to fit in with the overall divine plan, if we are to fulfill our purpose in this incarnation.

After screening many books and leaders of various cults and sects – some claiming divine guidance and unction, but none stacking up to what I perceived as the whole truth – I felt the urge to return to Sedona, Arizona, a spiritual center that I had visited several times before. Although Charles and I had lived in Phoenix and on the Colorado River near Havasu, we had only spent one night together near Sedona. After his demise in Santa Barbara, California, where I was fortified by fond relatives and had no need for an automobile of my own, I experienced the urge to be completely independent. Feeling quite capable of looking after myself, I set out for Sedona. Oddly enough, most everyone I met in this seven-vortexial center asked how and why I had come to Sedona. There is a subtle reason for this inquiry....

In the dim ages past, another continent flourished here. Lemuria had its spiritual center in this area; but, after one of the many Earth Changes, most of the continent went down just as Atlantis did at the end of its epoch. A part of the eastern sector, however, did not sink. It was, like Atlantis, a crystalline civilization, so the pundits claim. Yet, many imperfections came into being which could not be contained in many lifetimes, so the civilization had to be decimated until the next pralaya. The anointed ones of Lemuria are now in incarnation. Like homing pigeons, they are returning in droves to act as a catalyst to a new order whose central vortex is still in Sedona's environs. These anointed ones are following the Hopi Indians, whose realm it more recently had been.

Every time I try to talk myself into leaving these parts for any reason, it seems that I am not allowed to. My system craves, among other things, its dry climate. With breath being the most important function of the body, clean air and a clear sky are necessities which most other cities lack. Fleecy white clouds against a sky-blue background lure me back even when I attempt to prolong coastal visits. But the most compelling magnet of all is the great central vortex.

20

SEDONA'S
SEVEN VORTICES

Here I lean on the knowledge of those who claim authority: Page Bryant, Dick Sutphen, and others — especially Mary Lou Keller, a Sedona resident for a score of years, a realtor and pastor of Sedona Church of Light. She, in her generosity, shares her knowledge and wisdom with those interested enough to inquire.

What is an Earth vortex? you may ask. It is a spiraling motion, whirling with suction in the center. It is a spiritual force penetrating upward or downward and effecting positive or negative activity. The especially high, benign frequencies, even without our knowing their source or identity, are what attracts people to Sedona. Indeed, when, many years ago, Charles and I parked our Silverstreak travel trailer within the environs of Sedona, the vibrations were perceptible. During the night I was conscious of a great upliftment, fantastic dreams, and upon arising I experienced an illumination. It was as though I had merged with a luminary of some kind. I now believe that we had parked near one of these vital vortices. Like many others, I have made the rounds to the areas known to be vortical, but I've never recaptured the same scintillating feeling as at the former place, which I cannot relocate.

·21·

CRYSTALS

Recently I attended an impressive seminar on Crystal Connections. Wishing that I knew more on the subject and having been attracted to the authors of the book, *Windows of Light*, arrangements were made to house Drs. Randall and Vicki Baer as guests on their next trip to Sedona. To study crystals firsthand, a traveling friend had stored a huge crystal weighing 210 pounds in my study, together with bells, gongs, and several other brass objects, each sounding a different tone. Sensitive persons have been known to respond to the clear tones sounded by a gong or similar object, which stimulated certain of their body centers to raise vibrations. Amidst this combination of crystal and copper, some people have been healed of certain body imbalances and others have claimed spiritual upliftment.

•22•

SECRETS
OF ENOCH

This chapter is dedicated to Dr. J.J. Hurtak's, *The Keys of Enoch*.[1] In *The Forgotten Books of Eden* is a long chapter entitled "The Secrets of Enoch." Here, Enoch is introduced as one who is mentioned briefly in the book of Genesis: "He walked with God, and pleased God, was taken up and did not see death." This manuscript was widely read in the temples until the New Testament was compiled around A.D. 300. Enoch, the seventh from Adam, was the father of Methuselah; Enoch's father was Jared, and Enoch's grandson was Noah of the flood legend.

What follows is a review of Enoch's teachings, which I originally wrote for publication in Borderland Research Journal:

In the study of *The 64 Keys of Enoch* we learned that the author of the 600-page book, a Doctor of Oriental Languages, and a devout seeker of Truth, prayed for enlightenment; whereupon Enoch, appeared before him saying, "Are you ready?"

Then a field of Light encompassed the neophyte and he

---

[1] *Dr. James J. Hurtak and his wife Desiree have formed the Academy for Future Science to help carry on their work. Beautifully printed, bound and illustrated copies of The Keys of Enoch are available for $49, postpaid, from P.O. Box FE, Los Gatos, CA 95013.*

was sped upward into the heavens. Dr. James J. Hurtak was shown that the major programming center for our Earth is a midway station of Arcturus serving the Galactic Council of the Father. He was shown the network and courts used by the spiritual brotherhoods who adjudicate decisions pertaining to the planets in our region of space.

Hurtak wrote, "I was taken from Arcturus through a series of tessellations which seemed to be of a different tight density, where multiple, saddle-shaped concentric fields intersected so that a threshold was formed running through the star space connected with Orion." From there he exchanged his coarser body for a body of Light where dwell the Brotherhoods of Light. Again he was introduced to the Archangel Metatron who took him into the presence of the Father in a great field of Light. This was through the door of Omega Orion and into the Pyramid of Living Light, the Throne, where the Ancient of Days presides.

Briefly, Hurtak was enabled to see and comprehend the Office of the Christ. He was told to prepare a scroll coded unto him from the divine Scroll of Light, explaining how the Seven Seals of Revelation will be broken as all measures of science, from the metaphysical to the biophysical to the astrophysical are attuned to a new spiritual revelation in the name of Ayer Asher Ayheh, I Am that I Am. This scroll will bring forth a new cosmology of unconsciousness in explaining how the space Brotherhood of Light will work with those of the human race who accept the promise of a new life in the myriad other universes.

In other words, the long-expected prophecy wherein Science and Religion will be unified is now being fulfilled and one day there will be a Theocracy in government. Not in our lifetime will this happen, but perhaps before this Aquarian Age ends.

How does this all come about? Through understanding the complexities of the Pyramid. Through mantras, which act as sound waves that instantly follow a network of grid systems in and on every dimension of space, enlightening the receptive minds intuitively as well as bringing higher frequencies to the areas through which it passes. We learn that the Earth is undergoing renewal along with humankind and hopefully will regain its proper positional angle at the equator.

THE GOLDEN ESSENCE OF LOVE

Before getting deeply into the 64 keys of the divine scroll that Hurtak was to give to the world as the New Age teaching, his consciousness was overcome with the essence of Cosmic Love. In love was the essence and Golden was the Tone. The space vehicle that bore him into the heavens with Enoch is called Merkabah in the Hebrew language, a type such as Enoch said was, "wheels within wheels" as described by Ezekiel. Merkabah is a celestial Light vehicle used by the Brotherhood to probe and reach the faithful in the many dimensions of the divine mind. The Merkabah can take on many forms of a brilliant briolette in the physical worlds. Hence its ability to appear and to disappear interchangeably, as has been reported by fortunate people here on Earth. The classification would definitely be ETHERIC, not especially interplanetary.

The principals in Enoch's teaching are Melchizedek, Metatron and the Archangel Michael, as well as Christ Jesus, Moses, and Elijah, who also were taken up in a Merkabah and did not see death. These great beings, as well as those in the Eastern doctrine, such as Buddha, Krishna, Lao Tse, Zoroaster and others, appear to form triangles or triads that cannot be destroyed by negative forces. The fallen hierarchies who have control of our third-dimensional world are now being set back or removed from their once static plane in the region of Ursa Major and Ursa Minor. The astral world is being cleansed and purified as great forward strides are occurring constantly.

BE AWARE OF YOUR HIGHER BODIES

The purpose of these teachings is to break the bonds that have chained humanity to the physical world of three dimensions and to acquaint us with the reality of Self in its Shekinah glory. We learn in these exalted teachings that we have been equipped with sheaths, or bodies, to use as we enter the higher reaches of Space. We own bodies of Electromagnetic, Epikinetic, Ekka, a Gematrian body of Inner Light and a Zohar body of Outer Light. As a matter of fact, our education has only been a surface teaching and before mankind can ever emerge from this endless round of rebirth he must lay hold of his higher self and bring the OVERSOUL into everyday consciousness.

As our consciousness lifts to the awareness of the higher powers — Thrones, Virtues, Principalities, Dominions, Orders of Angels and Archangels, and their functions — our bodies become more Light and we begin to use the holy Seraphim and Cherubim as messengers of Light. We begin to feel with this newly discovered body equipment, and through our Third Eye we become aware of pictographs of extensions of sight into more lofty forms of creation. The electromagnetic body gets a toning, the molecular structure begins to take a less ponderous feeling as if walking on air at times.

In the study of the 64 Keys we are learning a new dimension of Sound, Light and Color. We are leaving our old worn-out fields of materiality and learning how to balance our energy fields and to activate the crystals throughout the entire body. It is a new language of Light and Harmonics. We begin to feel the presence of the luminaries. They impart to our higher consciousness frequencies that connect the membrane and chemistry of our bodies with the celestial membrane of the universe.

This book of knowledge brings into focus all the missing elements that education has overlooked and implants it into our waking consciousness that we might know the heights, the depths and the expanded width of our Universe of Light in which we live and move and have our being. The Pyramid unfolds its carbon copy of the Atom, and through its grid system we learn that triangles are formed from this precise center of the Earth, to Megiddo, to Bathsheba, to Bethlehem, the place of birth, as it were, of the trifold nature of our humanity. We also learn of the sacred grids in Altea, America, as they correspond to those in China and Tibet as well as those connected to the Pyramid. The Moslem's holy city of Mecca is part of a triangle of grids now revealed as a black cube which the holy hierarchy is attempting to cover with a golden pyramid. The diresome prophecy of Armageddon is being canceled and reversed by the power of the Holy Language of Mantras aimed to lift up the Earth Vortexja in that region. The New Jerusalem spoken of in St. John's Revelation is surely in the making, the pattern of which is already established.[2]

"Hurtak has successfully bridged the gap between Science and Religion. The approach to the Mysteries of Space is from the Western Mystery tradition and its Topography of the Universe, the Tree of Life of the Qabala."[3]

This Tree of Life is from the Golden Dawn tradition of MacGregor Mathers, Aleister Crowley and Dion Fortune. Metatron, the Archangel of the First Ray of Power, is supposed to have inspired the first teachings of the Qabala. His position on the Tree is at the very top. The Seraphim of Mars are located on the Pillar of Severity and the Cherubim of the Moon are on the Central Pillar. The other Sephiroth on the Tree also have their angel forces, which are ready to be called into action when properly invoked – such as the Malachim of the Christ, called upon when doing healing work.

---

[2]*Reprinted with permission from the author's original publication in* Borderland Research Journal *(Nov. 1984 and Jan. 1985), available from P.O. Box 549, Vista, CA 92083-0549.*
[3]*Riley Crabb, Editor,* Boderland Research Journal, *see Note 2.*

THE TREE OF LIFE

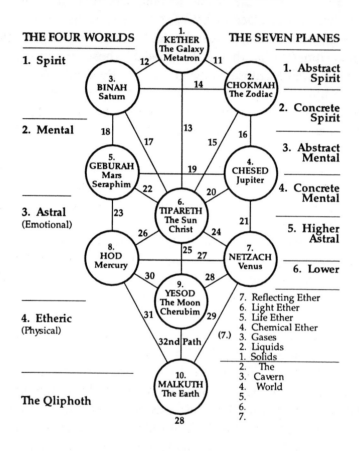

THE FOUR WORLDS

1. Spirit

2. Mental

3. Astral
(Emotional)

4. Etheric
(Physical)

The Qliphoth

THE SEVEN PLANES

1. Abstract
   Spirit

2. Concrete
   Spirit

3. Abstract
   Mental

4. Concrete
   Mental

5. Higher
   Astral

6. Lower

7. Reflecting Ether
6. Light Ether
5. Life Ether
4. Chemical Ether
3. Gases
2. Liquids
1. Solids

2. The
3. Cavern
4. World
5.
6.
7.

1.
KETHER
The Galaxy
Metatron

3.
BINAH
Saturn

2.
CHOKMAH
The Zodiac

5.
GEBURAH
Mars
Seraphim

4.
CHESED
Jupiter

6.
TIPARETH
The Sun
Christ

8.
HOD
Mercury

7.
NETZACH
Venus

9.
YESOD
The Moon
Cherubim

10.
MALKUTH
The Earth

12 11 14 13 15 16 17 18 19 20 21 22 23 24 25 26 27 28 30 31 29 32nd Path (7.) 28

Returning from his celestial euphoria (Merkabah), Dr. Hurtak lost his neophyte status, as had Swedenborg 200 years previously when he passed into the higher dimensions in full consciousness. Dr. Hurtak covered actual spatial interviews with entities such as Enoch, Melchizedek and the Archangel Metatron, formulator of the higher sciences. He became acquainted with some of the hosts of heaven, even with the Archangels Michael, Raphael, Gabriel and others not in our galactic field.

He also met with many in superstar universes such as Sirius, Orion and the Pleiades, as well as with their rulers. We must admit that having such experiences is a rare occurrence, seldom given to anyone within any millennium and rarely in the same manner. Fortunately, for inquisitive minds, both Swedenborg and Dr. Hurtak were able to record as well as publish their celestial findings. The world is now conceivably richer from having read and studied these revealed experiences.

The scribe – in this instance, Dr. Hurtak – reminds me that we are currently in a cosmic countdown and that the time is much later than we believe. In a recent class study in Sedona, our knowledgeable instructor gave us a preview, stressing the importance of Giza pyramid in relation to survival on our planet:

"Before this great enigmatic structure was dismantled, or rather deactivated, at about the time of the Exodus, ancient records speak of a capstone, possibly a magnetized crystal which served as a beacon of pulsating energy – a homing device. As for the structure itself, the pyramid or rather "pyro-mid," translated as "fire in the center," involved a cosmic technology little understood by our modern scientists and physicists. In fact, it is quite beyond ordinary comprehension, as it involves light techniques connected with the stars as well as a massive grid system in which our planet plays but an infinitesimal part."

"From the standpoint of modern physics, the Giza pyramid is an enlarged duplicate of the carbon atom. According to Enoch, it is also the magnetic model of the human body as well as the mathematics of the human heartbeat. It resembles something like a biorhythm chart etched in stone. You can also find crystalline, pyramidal particles in human blood, which contains all the mathematics of DNA - RNA that make physical life possible on this planet. It is the lower chemistry of star creations. Indeed, we are learning that the pyramidal [pyro-mid] model in all of its varied aspects is vital to our very existence."

"Situated exactly in the geophysical center of the land mass of the Earth, this miracle in stone, according to Master Enoch, also contains an extremely complex star code which, as already noted, involved the human evolutionary process. This is all in accord with the overall Cosmic Plan in which the pyramid radiates and pulsates invisible shafts of light in the direction of Orion and the Pleiades, our central Sun. Few realize that from these two beacons of Light Intelligence came forth the Adamic race as we know it, on the Seventh Ray of Creation."

Briefly, the influence of new magnetic wavelengths now reaching our planet, both stimulating and changing old biomagnetic forces in our bodies, are being felt by almost everyone. Those on the left-hand path appear to be adversely affected. Others appear to be stimulated and are given the vision of a bright future when the final conflict ceases. The changes now going on may cause geophysical changes, as the great tectonic plates of the Earth begin to shift in relation to specific star points and radiation centers divided into twelve segments. We are told by geologists that the planet's poles have in past ages reversed several times according to some rhythmic cycle. At the present time, we are at the close of a 6,000-year cycle.

Faith in the hierarchies and heavenly hosts, as well as in the ancient wisdom of the Qabala (Kabbala) — which only the chosen of the chosen are allowed to see and understand — is but one of the truths explained in this teaching. The Qabala reveals how our universe is governed by the wisdom and glories of still higher universes, whose scientific teachings are given in every age in order that the species on this and other planets can find their resurrection into the higher evolution of life.

Enoch explained that mankind, in the foreseeable future, through advanced DNA - RNA coding, will have the ability to overcome death. "Throughout our present redemptive age 'the spiritual Israel,' exemplified through the work of Enoch, Elijah, and Jesus, proved that physical ascension is possible in this dimension or reality for all the world to experience."[4]

By means of changing his chemical and atomic structure, man will one day learn to use his higher body for multidimensional travel, thus freeing himself from the limitations of time and space, all of which conform to cosmic law.

Our species is a wondrous miracle. Why should we not try to fathom its genius, especially with the possibility of being rescued by Merkabah if the Earth Changes become too violent? These elusive, self-contained vehicles, some 50 miles in length, should be able to accommodate a large number of Earth beings, should the need arise.[5]

This is but a brief capsulation of this 600-page book. It does not begin to unfold the deep substance of this glorious Book of Knowledge, as Dr. Hurtak refers to it, in which prophetic events are about to take place and mankind receives instruction to escape most of the travail and trauma that is apt to follow in the wake of these Earth Changes which the seismologists are also predicting. There is no doubt of the planet's atmospheric and water pollution, but our Earth itself is in great need of cleansing. Some areas on the globe may be safe, and some may be safer than others. Rather than react to this information in an alarmist fashion, we do have the option of gearing our personal preparation for the event to a higher dimension.

[4]The Keys of Enoch, *Key 3-1-9, p.545. Quoted with the author's permission.*
[5]*A detailed description of life aboard a Merkabah 10 miles in diameter can be found in one of the earliest contactee books, Orfeo Angelucci's* Son of the Sun, *first published in 1959 and now long out of print.*

•23•

BIOSATELLITES, MERKABAH AND SUPER UFO'S

Wwhat is a Merkabah?" you may ask. The glossary of *The Keys of Enoch* reads: "Divine Light Vehicle used by the Masters to probe and reach the faithful in the many dimensions of the Divine Mind." The Merkabah (ethereal UFO) can take on many forms of a brilliant briolette in the physical worlds.[1] Some are biosatellites almost as large as the tiny moons of Jupiter or Saturn, on which 10,000 or more persons could live a lifetime. Some of these biosatellites might be cruising our planet now, totally invisible to us; or, the "pilots" can materialize the vehicles, in which case they may be seen and reported as Mother Ships.

This is what I believe Charles and I saw in space when we slept out beneath the sky in July, 1952. Whatever it may have been, it was reported by a military observers miles from us in Borrego Valley, California. We saw tiny disks going in and out of this ship in rhythmic motion for hours on end, while the vehicle was more or less stationary. It baffled our minds. One of the disks appeared to be what has been de-scribed as a flying saucer. Years earlier, while Charles and I

---

[1] *Ezekiell:4-28*

were cruising in the Pacific Ocean on the motorship *Janette R*, we looked up at 4:00 p.m. on June 12, 1926 to see a magnetically charged disk fly overhead and zap me with its radiation.

It penetrated my heart with a fire that burned for weeks on end. The pain, not excruciating, was more like a "love vibration" – a contact from space a full 20 years before pilot Arnold reported a string of disks flying in formation in the Northwest. "Oh," as Hamlet said, "there are more things than our philosophy dreams of!" Never were words more true than when applied to a celestial science about which we know scarcely anything.

My sense is that this experience has had something to do with my longevity. With the radiation came an opening up of my mental processes, or perhaps it was an awakening of my spiritual senses. I am reminded of the five sheaths of higher frequencies that, through non-use, have atrophied and need reawakening. Now I imagine that this is what happened; but at the time that the disk shot overhead, it really blew my mind. The two great beings who materialized in the tack room when I was five years old could have been spacemen although they actually appeared more like the wise men who use flying carpets.

Now we may proceed farther into the dimensions of the luminaries – the angels, the archangels, the heavenly hosts – and try to visualize how these celestial UFOs function. They appear in a multitude of forms. Sometimes they are seen as pure energy in lightning flashes around a person's head, or as if exuding from one's eyes in a brilliant flash of miniature lightning–jagged streaks of spiderweb lengths zigzagging in soft cadences. They can continue to materialize for hours, as reminders of a holy presence, and always leave one with the consciousness of a high frequency.

Merkabah is called the Vehicle of Vehicles when concentrated in a solidified form, but the light substance is the same regardless of its concentration – part of the Divine Economy of Spiritual Laws. Merkabah is a vehicle which can take on any membrane of color appearance to correspond with the seer and guide him or her into other experiences of creation. It controls time translation and hooks up dimensions of light. Occasionally, lower, negative UFO craft are prevented from coming into our Earth aura by the Merkabah watchers. And through the Holy Spirit, earthlings can be given knowledge to understand how a divine connection can be made with Merkabah's celestial synch. The power and direction of Merkabah proceeds directly from the Mind which is in conjunction with God. This Mind of a high being literally operates, controls and stabilizes it at all times so that when it passes by, it heralds a divine message from the Father.

This is what I felt when that disk zoomed over our cruise ship in the Pacific Ocean. For two days the captain complained that the ship's instruments would not work and that he could not find the longitude of where we were sailing. In the end, we learned that we were over 100 miles off course. It took years for me to figure out what had happened: UFO electromagnetism!

·24·

BASICS OF LONGEVITY

Non-aging and longevity, while related, are not in-
ter changeable. Now that I can speak in the past
tense, having proved my philosophy of keeping the faculties
intact with no sign of senility, you can rely on the
techniques given. Pick out the aspect that suits your
particular needs: philosophy, exercise, nutrition, even selec-
tive travel can help. Change is essential once in a while.
Expand your borders, if not within mundane territories,
certainly skyward into astronomy.

Astrology was once a science. Although it still is, the
calendars have certainly gotten fouled up. One astrologer I
know, who was quite adept, no longer sets up charts since
our time clock has been speeded up until we are almost nine
years ahead of schedule. Nevertheless, there are those like
Prince Hirendra, an astrologer in the Eastern tradition, who
say that without constructing a chart to comply with past
lives, we have no foundation on which to build. However,
much can be deduced from it, the study simply does not fill
my present needs as much as it did my past needs. For
others, this is not so. Astrology may be exactly what could
give you a lift to a place you may want to be; it could help

you to better understand yourself and your relationships with others.

I am presently experimenting with supplemental foods, though I still take vitamins C and E frequently. Chlorophyll, together with a blend of marine algae and alfalfa juice concentrate, appears to put a little bounce into old bones. Organic seafoods can be just the missing element in your diet if you live inland and do not eat enough seafood. I also use sea salt in cooking and powdered kelp in salads as supplementary sources of iodine. Not too much at a time, if you wish to retain taste appeal!

People ask me if I believe in plastic surgery and facial peels. Yes, for some individuals, but not for others. I wish that I had had a peel when I was younger. My sister had a facelift 10 years ago, and it was the greatest thing that could have happened to her. It has held up well, and she looks young and feels young because of it. Others have not fared so well. For example, my niece had a lift which became infected, leaving a strange, unnatural look around her eyes.

A quick substitute for Hauser's Seven-Oil Facial Treatment: Mix together vitamin E oil, castor oil, and olive oil for a late night or early morning application. Then rub a skin gel over the oils to help them penetrate more deeply. Keep the skin moist for an hour or two. This is not the Gaylord Hauser formula, but it is almost as beneficial!

The best facial scrub I ever tested was not exactly a scrub, but rather a Slo-Peel, by Jeneatte Coburn Cosmetics, Inc. of Palm Beach, Florida. It took away the leathery look and left my skin softer and more transparent.

Recently, after having tried dozens of other promising brands, I have found that Hauser's Seven-Oils recipe for keeping the face lubricated and wrinkle free merits a second look. If your skin is dry, or if you live in a dry climate, it is almost impossible to keep facial skin from forming wrinkles. To improve on Cleopatra's formula, mix in a measuring cup: 3T safflower oil, 3T sesame oil, 2T sunflower oil, 2T avocado oil,

1T peanut oil, 1T olive oil, 1T wheat germ oil. If desired, add 5 drops of rose geranium or your favorite perfume.

In the quest to remain youthful, one should also understand the importance of normal blood circulation. If the arteries get clogged with cholesterol, then the whole system runs down, often leading to gallstone formation. Although the following herbs can be helpful, – one should always consult a physician prior to attempting treatment. Herbs that I have found helpful are: Silica Alta Sil-x, an extract of horsetail herbs; and Hawthorn Combination, which contains Hawthorn berries, cayenne, and soya lecithin.

For those who do not engage in active sports or regular exercise, it is a good idea to use an electric vibrator on the body and head. I have a Flexi-bed with a vibrator attachment that I often use. I also use a weak facial and head vibrator to stimulate the scalp follicles and to encourage circulation near the ears, eyes, and temples. Remember the back of your neck too, and the base of the spine. While stimulating the head area, be sure to recognize that nearby are three important ductless glands: the pituitary, pineal, and hypothalamus. Keep these tiny but powerful head vortexes circulated and you will be forever young. But exercise caution: Do not use a powerful vibrator, as these glands need only mild stimulation.

•25•

ANCIENT SCRIPTS

How fortunate we are that so much ancient wisdom has been recorded and preserved for us. Here, for example, is an excerpt from the *Stanzas of Dyzan,* one of the oldest known Sanskrit scripts: "The Primordial Seven, the first seven breaths of the Dragon of Wisdom, produce in their turn from the circumgyrating breaths, the Fiery Whirlwind." This stanza alludes to the sky objects a "messengers of their will"–their creators being the Lords of Flame – using Fohat (the steed) to form the Germs of the Wheels. "Fohat takes five strides and collects fiery dust and builds a winged wheel for the Holy Ones and their armies."

In ancient India at the time of Rama, these wheels were called Tirupure, a Sanskrit word translated as "moving air castles." Valex is the name given for biosatellites Atlantis, according to *Dweller on Two Planets* by Phylos, which was published near the end of the last century. Phylos, who lived there before the flood, claimed that transportation was propelled by incorporating the forces of nature taken from the ether. The narrative claims that our continent, America, was just one of the dominions of Atlantis and that these airships or valex, soared everywhere on the planet. This was long before the occurrence of sky flights. What is more, Phylos described television that showed the pilot where he was going. As a young woman reading this before we had planes or TV, it almost made me daft. So you see, there is wisdom to be had in lifting your thoughts skyward.

◆26◆

DIVINE GOVERNMENT

Who are the hosts of Heaven? Besides Angels and Archangels, there are Principalities and Powers, Thrones, Virtues, Dominions. Each of the Archangels has a name and a task, and there are also special functions of the Cherubim and Seraphim. My brother, who is a pastor, dotes so much on Jesus that he thinks everyone and everything else is extra baggage. How can we ignore the cooperation and work of the many Hosts? When we are aware of this array of power, we can be assured that our invocations will be recorded and that our prayers will be answered.

A wise man once said, "The great wheel of life rolls ever on and on in space 'round its orbit unmoved by time. Races come and fall, and in the great human life struggle, one short individual existence is but a breath – a fleeting zephyr in the whole. Mankind hath no fate except past deeds; no hell but what he makes and no heaven too high for those whose passions sleep subdued."

Teachers have a powerful influence over the minds of their pupils. For instance, one teacher I had before I was 10 years old started the afternoon class by having us memorize mottoes. To this day, when I wake up and would like to be lazy,

I quote, "Let us be up and doing with a heart for any fate, still achieving, still pursuing, learn to labor and to wait."

And sometimes, when I am carelessly out of something and think of asking a neighbor for the item, one of Shakespeare's old sayings comes to mind, "Neither a borrower nor a lender be, for the lender often loses both itself and friend and borrowing dulls the edge of husbandry." I thank my teachers for their mottoes, which have helped me to retain friends I might have otherwise lost. As for lending, I must admit that once in a blue moon I have indulged, for Yogananda cautioned me never to turn aside anyone when help is needed.

Benjamin Franklin is said to have written, "A man is not completely born until he dies. Why then should we grieve that a new child is born among the immortals? We are spirits. That bodies should be lent to us while they can afford us pleasure, assist us in acquiring knowledge or in doing good to our fellow creatures, as a kind and benevolent act of God; when they become unfit for these purposes and afford us pain instead of pleasure, instead of an aid become an encumbrance, it is equally kind and benevolent that a way is provided by which we may get rid of them. Death is that way."

Pythagoras, known as the Father of Philosophy, poetically described rebirth when he said:

> *Death hath not the power the immortal part to slay*
> *Which, when its present body turns to clay,*
> *Seeks a fresh home, and with undiminished might*
> *Inspires another frame with life and light.*

Walt Whitman, in speaking of spiritual realms and our faculties, wrote, "I do not doubt that interiors have interiors, and exteriors have their exteriors, and the eyesight, other eyesight and that hearing, another hearing and the voice, another voice." To know God is to know all worlds, all saviors, and how you fit into the whole scheme of things.

The fountain of youth is within. Since time began, man has searched outside himself for rejuvenation. He has explored witchcraft, magic potions, and miracle drugs. But the only place that rejuvenation is possible is within oneself. The time to start is now, regardless of what your chronological age may be. Ultimately, everyone has a right to feel young and healthy for as long as he or she lives on this Earth.

Often unsuspected are our inner realms of empowerment. Did you know that the planet is circled and crisscrossed with grids and ley lines? This is true not only in our three-dimensional world, but also below and above and "within" on various levels. You may ask, what is a "grid"? A grid is formed by the latitude and longitude lines interconnecting at certain points and forming a pattern on which a map can be read. Psalm 16:6 reveals, "The lines are fallen unto me in pleasant places; yea I have a goodly heritage." Sound waves follow these grid lines and can be carried to great distances. To one who can see within, these grids look like electrified spider threads, not in the form of a web, but mostly geometrical. Everyone has his own grids, just as he has vortices and chakras, even if they are unknown. Such grids are necessary in order to participate in the law of transfer of energy. Adhesion, cohesion, and magnetism are the principles of levitation.

Remember that the consciousness of God that sustains the universe also sustains man, and man is within the conscious act which sustains the universe. The important factors in being forever young include both the outer garment and the inner garment — exercise and nutrition, and also one's attitude toward life and God and our fellow beings. Paramount to everything else, learn who you are. Be good to yourself; but, if you do something unworthy, forgive yourself and do not harbor guilt. Cry to your whole heart, to your supreme self, and never give up until your oversoul claims your ego-personality and supplants it with the Song of Immortality!

·27·

PROBERT/YADA
ON SEX

In the decade of the fifties, we were invited by a member of the Inner Circle to attend a gathering at the apartment of Mark Probert in San Diego. Mark disliked the connotation of "medium", so he insisted that we refer to his special gift for channeling entities from beyond the pale as "telegnosis". Yada di Shi'ite, who claimed to be from a civilization that was wiped out some 500,000 years ago, was the most enlightened of the dozen or more masterful entities who issued forth from Mark Probert's throat and lips.

This esoteric group also published a journal called *Round Robin*, later known as the *Borderland Scientific Research Journal*. They also saw to it that the wisdom of Yada was recorded and later published in a book entitled *Yada Speaks*. *The Magic Bag*, a subsequent book by Mark, is now most likely out of print, but it contains the reports of the other illumined entities who spoke through him.

Valuable insights are offered by Yada on the subjects of sexuality and aging: "No one should stop, or be unable, or settle for – what is the word – impotence? No one need suffer it. It is not the normal thing, that because we reach a certain age, now we are done. It is coming from mental blocks, from experiences you have had that have done something to you mentally against it."

And, continuing: "Love does not bind. Love holds together by itself. By its own nature. It is made of silken cords, it gives much latitude for motion. Now, if you knew how to use this energy to help your fellow man, he would be more satisfied with his life. To give of your vital energies to someone you love, that is glorifying yourself creatively. But when you misuse it or give it to someone you do not love, you devitalize yourself."

A wise man of our family often dissertated on the constitution of the sex force. He said that it is the motivating force in this physical existence, excluding the sex act itself. He knew a man who had deliberately made himself a eunuch because of his false belief that the sexual act was a sin. Prior to this, he had been a vital and healthy man; afterward, although continuing to express a great deal of love for everyone, he became terminally ill and, bereft of this natural force, died at quite an early age.

Bless your God-given energy, use it for creative purposes, but do not give it away. Controlled use of this vital energy will keep you young. Misuse withers the creative spirit.

Yada's teachings were profound, but only a few groups had the privilege of Mark Probert's presence. Following the Inner Circle, a more dynamic group in Palm Springs recognized what a prize they had in both Mark and Yada. Later, a great many of Yada's tapes were included in a book by Lehmann Hisey, entitled *The Keys of Inner Space.*[1]

[1]*This book was published by The Julian Press, Inc., 150 Fifth Ave., New York, NY 10011. A second printing of this fine work will soon be issued by Crown Publications, at the same address.*

·28·

KEYS OF ENOCH:
THE ASCENSION PROCESS
EMERALD TABLETS, ENDURING

During this special changeover from the old Piscean dispensation to this New Order of enlightenment it is good to know that there are a few permanent things one can count on. All of the old, worn-out, false illusions have been surreptitiously swept away. And it is a good thing. Thank Jove, the bearer of good tidings! One of the glorious things remaining in our consciousness is ancients records, artifacts and timeless scrolls. These are instruments of cohesion from past to present. Among such precious information is the truly ancient Emerald Tablets found under the old Temple of the Sun at Palenque, Yucatan. Some scribes put them at 3600 B.C. Others think they date back to the golden Age and beyond. Nevertheless, it is the wisdom the tablets contain that increases their worth.

Why are these priceless Emerald Tablets so significant to this New Order, one might ask? The answer is that their contents permit us to see great, meaningful things in perspective. Translated into modern language, it brings knowledge of Lemuria, Atlantis and Egypt together consecutively, speaking about spaceships and how longevity was retained.

More than that, it tells you how to die gracefully when your work is done. The world needs to accept an all-new formula for dying: LIFE is the answer for that. Actually, there is NO DEATH — unless, of course, one prefers the grave. Jesus said that Death is the last enemy to be overcome. So even back in the Golden Age, one had a choice to live or exit gracefully.

Hermes Trismegistus of the Egyptians is regarded as the same soul as the ancient Atlantean Thoth. Let us just regard them as continuing counterparts. Now let us take a glimpse of a few excerpts from these remarkable Emerald Tablets:

"I, Thoth, the Atlantean, give you of my wisdom; give you of my knowledge: give of my power; freely give to the children of men. Give that which they too might have wisdom to shine through the world. Wisdom is power and power is wisdom, one with each other, perfecting the whole...Exalt not thy speech above men, for thou shalt be brought lower than the dust. The wise man lets not his heart overflow, but keeps silence his mouth...All eyes do not see with the same vision an object that appears of one form and to a different eye of another, as also the infinite fire, changing from color to color, from day to day." (From Vol. 1)

"Oft dream I of buried Atlantis, Lost to the ages that have passed into night. Aeon on aeon thou existed, in beauty, a light shining bright through the darkness of night. I, Thoth, have ever sought wisdom. There on the throne, beheld I the dweller, clothed with the Light and flashing with fire. Down I knelt before that great wisdom, feeling the Light flowing through me in waves. Heard I then the voice of the dweller, Oh darkness come into the Light. Each soul on Earth that loosens its fetters shall soon be made free from the bondage of night." (From Vol. 5)

As the waters engulfed Atlantis, orders were given: "Take thou, O Thoth, all your wisdom, take all your records, take all your magic and go thou forth as a teacher of men...Then gathered I the sons of Atlantis into the space ship. I brought all my records...Up we rose on wings of the morning. Fled we to the land of the children of Khem [Egypt]. Deep 'neath the rocks I buried my space ship, waiting the time when men might be free. Over the space ship I erected a marker in the form of a lion, yet like unto man; there 'neath the image rests yet, forth my space ship to be brought when need shall arise." (From Vol. 5)

·29·

CRYSTAL POWER: SARI

A lthough I had met Sari (Lucille McNames) briefly three years before, our great shared connection was with Yogananda, whose presence was revealed to her from the higher reaches of consciousness and by whom she was taught for four years. My acquaintance with this great soul, Paramhansa Yogananda, was much earlier, when he was in the flesh, especially at the Hermitage near Encinitas located within the radius of our ranch.

Following are excerpts from her book Startling Revelations, expressing the relationship of crystal power to youthfulness and immortality:

Did you know that crystal light is so potent that it can heal the world, or blow it up? Three-dimensional [3-D] activity in crystals is the EXTERNAL EXPRESSION OF LIGHT. Activity in four-dimensional [4-D] crystals is INTERNAL EXPRESSION OF LIGHT. Many moons ago those Beings whom you call UFOnauts buried relevant data in caves, in mountains, and in other remote areas where man cannot find them. The Brothers had foresight, knowing that earthlings would have need of more potent light for their higher frequency body during a new age. Your Cosmic Brothers often land and recharge these crystals. How? With their own crystalline energy. When the time is right, universal crystals shall be accidentally discovered. Many of you do not believe that gods carefully guard precious gold, silver, stones, and gems in your Earth, in your mountains, and in giant caves under the seas....

It is true that highly evolved crystals liquify into Divine Fire. White atoms doeth the work. When light is solidified on Earth, Light becomes frozen Light. As crystals evolve, they thaw and become Divine Fire. When crystallographers delve more deeply into crystal light, they will discover miracles....

God is the power in laser light! God is Essence [that] you know as lasered light, but as we write this, man still knows so very little about power in laser beams. Much more will be revealed in the not-too-distant future. Of course, the new healing will be accomplished in just seconds, with a prism through crystal. It is vitally necessary to refract the cosmic rainbow-balanced color-tones through the   crystal. The great central sun charges crystals perpetually. Also, laser light can penetrate not only the total body, but the four mind areas as well. So you now see how it is possible for medical science to practice a so-called new art with prismed crystals.

There exists now, in the etheric, a sophisticated radionic computer that shall prove to be an infallible diagnostic tool, that shall disclose any ailment in any of the body and in the four mind levels. If surgery is needed, proper color rays crystallized in lasered rays shall eliminate surgery. Healing shall be fantastic. Even after what usually is serious surgery [the individual] shall heal sometimes in just a few minutes or a few hours at the most. Lasered rays shall reach all parts of mind and body and align [the] same.

Light waves that have been converted from sounds in the etheric realms do form image patterns, so this is how communication works. In the etheric realms, remember, there is no past or future. Universal law works in timeless and spaceless mind zones, so to speak. But there exists time and space in lower realms, of course.[1]

---

[1]*Excerpted with permission by Sari, from* Startling Revelations. *For ordering information, see Recommended Reading.*

◆30◆

ARISE
AND AWAKEN

As I write this last chapter, the October sun hesitatingly rises behind filmy clouds against the rugged outline of the red rocks, as if defying all other beautiful morns. In the foreground, the expanse of the Coconino Forest blends with the manmade edifices as the misty gray turns to green. Simultaneously, the cerise sky that heralded the first glimpse of dawn retreats into a purplish-pinkish froth. Above this world spectacular, the bowl of heaven appears cobalt blue, gradually fading into an anthem of colors, and finally resolving into a clear blue sky. How can one sustain such beauty after the Sun gathers its light and spreads it over a sleeping universe? The mind's eye records it all.

So with life also – what it was and what it can be – it is all ours to enjoy, even unto the illusory end, illusory because there is never an end, as there was never a beginning. The sunrise is there, but one needs to arise for it to be seen.

God is in the midst of it all, telling us of His love, showing an appreciative world His boundless splendor. Even to dim, uncaring eyes, this glory is not withheld. Therefore, arise and awaken and be forever young!

◆APPENDIX◆

THE RITES OF REJUVENATION

A British officer stationed in the foothills of the Himalayas in India learned of a sect of lamas who never seemed to get old. Legend had it that they held the secret of longevity. Colonel Bradford himself had aged rapidly and, upon retirement, searched them out and entered their lamasery. When he emerged two years later, he was an entirely new man. He was so delighted with his transformation that he wanted to share his secret with the whole world. He began teaching the techniques to large numbers of people in India and London. Eventually he came to the United States and taught the Rites here.

A friend named Peter Kelder, who knew Colonel Bradford before and after his transformation, wrote a booklet setting forth the *Rites of Rejuvenation*, which was copyrighted in 1939. Twenty- five years later, after being out of print for more than two decades, the copyright expired, and another printing was made by Borderland Sciences Research Foundation. The second printing has proved to be just as popular as the first.

According to Colonel Bradford's report, there are seven Psychic Vortexes in the body. Vortex A is located within the forehead; Vortex B is located in the posterior part of the brain; Vortex C is in the region of the throat at the base of the neck; Vortex D is located in the right side of the body above the waistline; Vortex E is located in the reproductive anatomy and is directly connected with Vortex C, in the throat. Vortexes F and G are located one in each knee.

These Psychic Vortexes revolve at great speed. When all are revolving at high speed and at the same rate of speed, the body is in perfect health. When one or more of them slow down, old age, loss of power, and senility set in.[1]

Rite Number One

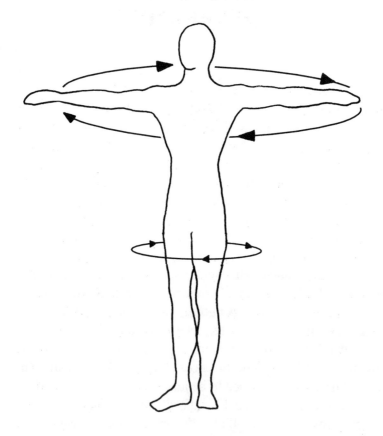

---

[1]*The following diagrams are excerpted and reproduced with permission from* The Five Rites of Rejuvenation *by Peter Kelder, copyright © 1939.*

The first Rite is a simple one. It is for the express purpose of speeding up the Vortexes. When we were children, we used it in our play.

Stand erect with arms outstretched, horizontal with the shoulders. Now, spin around left to right until you become slightly dizzy. In other words, if you were to place a clock face up on the floor, you would turn in the same way the hands are moving.

At first, the average adult will only be able to spin around about a half dozen times until he or she becomes dizzy enough to want to sit or lie down. This is just what you should do, too. In the beginning, practice this rite only to the point of slight dizziness. As time passes and your vortexes become more rapid in movement through this and other Rites, you will be able to practice it to a greater extent.

Never carry this whirling exercise to excess. While the whirling dervishes may spin around hundreds of times, greater benefit is obtained by restricting the spins to about a dozen. The object of Rite Number One is to stimulate all the Vortexes to action.

Rite Number Two

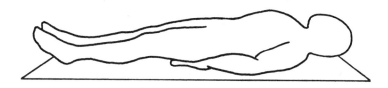

First Position

Rite Number Two

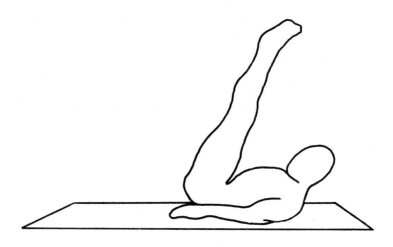

Second Position

Rite Number Two is for further stimulating to action the Seven Vortexes. It is even simpler than the first Rite.

Lie flat on your back on the floor or a bed. If you are practicing on the floor, work on a rug or blanket folded several times so that your body will not come in contact with the cold floor.

Now, place your hands flat down alongside your hips. Fingers should be kept close together, with the fingertips of each hand turned slightly toward one another. Then, raise your feet until your legs are straight up. If possible, let your feet extend back a bit toward your head, but do not bend your knees. Slowly lower feet to the floor, and for a moment allow all muscles to relax. Then perform this Rite a second time.

Rite Number Three

Rite Number Three should be practiced immediately after Rite Number Two. It, too, is very simple, and particularly effective in speeding up Vortexes E, D, and C – especially E.

Kneel on your "prayer rug" mat, or blanket, and place hands on thighs. Now, lean forward as far as possible with head inclined so that your chin rests on your chest. Next, lean backward as far as possible, at the same time lifting your head and throwing it back as far as it will go. Then bring your head up along with your body. Leaning forward again, repeat this Rite.

Rite Number Four

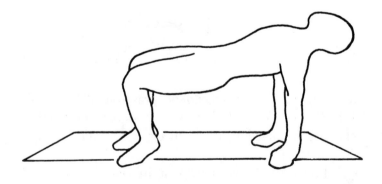

The first time I tried this, it seemed very difficult. But, after one week, it was as simple to perform as any of the others.

Sit on the "prayer rug" with your feet stretched out in front of you. Then place your hands alongside your body. Now, raise your body and bend your knees so that your legs, from the knees down, are practically vertical. Your arms will also be vertical, while your body will be horizontal from shoulders to knees. (Before pushing up to the horizontal position, your chin should be tucked well down, touching your chest. Then, as you raise your body, allow your head to drop gently backward as far as it will go.) Return to a sitting position and relax for a moment before repeating the procedure.

When your body is pressed up to the complete horizontal position, tense every muscle in the body. This will tend to stimulate Vortexes F, G, E and C.

Rite Number Five

The best way to perform this Rite is to place your hands on the floor, about two feet apart. Then, with your legs stretched out to the rear — feet also about two feet apart — push your body, especially your hips, up as far as possible, rising on your toes and hands. At the same time, bring your head all the way down until your chin touches your chest.

Next, allow your body to come slowly down to a "sagging" position. Bring head up, drawing it back as far as possible.

After a few weeks, or when you have become quite proficient in this movement, let the body drop from its highest position to a point almost but not quite touching the floor. Tense your muscles for a moment while your body is at its highest point, and again at its lowest point. Before the end of the first week, the average person usually finds that this Rite is one of the easiest to perform.[2]

[2]*The Five Rites described reveal only the salient features. For the entire booklet, send $3 to Borderland Sciences Research Foundation, P.O. Box 549, Vista, CA 92083-0549.*

◆ABOUT THE AUTHOR◆

Born on December 30, 1895 in the Cherokee Strip, Oklahoma Territory, Gladys Iris Clark has traveled and studied extensively. She shared a love for archaeology with her husband Charles, and together they explored Egypt, Greece, South America, New Zealand, the Orient and the Near East.

Over the years, Iris has developed a deep and abiding interest in great world teachings. Emanuel Swedenborg, Yognanda, *The Keys of Enoch*, Tai Chi, Tibetan Yoga, and St. Hildegard are among the inspirations from age-old wisdom that have had a profound influence on her life and her work.

A prolific writer and skilled researcher, Iris has had her work published in two London-based journals and in *American West* magazine. She has earned a Eugene Field award for her work on the Andes. She is also the author of the book **Long-Line Riders**.

Iris was possibly one of the first ladies to be zapped by a UFO. This occurred on board ship of "Janette R," June 13, 1926 while cruising to La Paz, Mexico. "The high energy burned in my heart for six weeks," marvels Iris.

Iris currently lives in Sedona, Arizona, where she is sometimes referred to as The Crystal Lady. The 210-pound crystal in her study draws numerous visitors. As she says, "It is a pulsating crystal, of the healing type. But its primary purpose is to be a catalyst in a triad of huge crystals in this area, creating a forcefield for levitation – not only to assist in aiding the planet, but also to lift the consciousness of the entities living on it."

RECOMMENDED
◆READING◆

Baer, Randall N., and Vikki Vittitow Baer. **Windows of Light: Using Quartz Crystals as Tools for Self-Transformation**. Harper and Row, 1984.

Bailey, Alice and the Tibetan Master, Djwhal Khul. **Ponder On This**. Lucia Press, Ltd., 1971.

Hisey, Lehmann. **The Keys To Inner Space: An Open-Ended Guide to Occultism, Metaphysics and the Transcendental**. New York: The Julian Press, 1974.

Hurtak, J.J. **The Book of Knowledge: The Keys of Enoch**. 1977. The Academy for Future Science, P.O. Box FE, Los Gatos, CA 95030.

Newhouse, Flower A. **Natives of Eternity**. J.F. Rowney Press, 1937. This and other books by the author can be obtained by writing to her at Route 5, Box 206, Escondido, CA 92025.

Probert, Mark. **The Magic Bag**. Available from The Inner Circle Kethra E'Da Foundation, Inc., P.O. Box 1722, San Diego, CA 92112.

Sari. **Startling Revelations**. 1979. Available from Lucille McNames, 205 Sunset Drive, Box 48, Sedona, AZ 86336.